Samuel French Acting Edition

The Odd Couple

by Neil Simon

SAMUELFRENCH.COM   SAMUELFRENCH.CO.UK

ISBN 978-0-573-61331-9

www.SamuelFrench.com
www.SamuelFrench.co.uk

FOR PRODUCTION ENQUIRIES

UNITED STATES AND CANADA
Info@SamuelFrench.com
1-866-598-8449

UNITED KINGDOM AND EUROPE
Plays@SamuelFrench.co.uk
020-7255-4302

Each title is subject to availability from Samuel French, depending upon country of performance. Please be aware that *THE ODD COUPLE* may not be licensed by Samuel French in your territory. Professional and amateur producers should contact the nearest Samuel French office or licensing partner to verify availability.

MUSIC USE NOTE

IMPORTANT BILLING AND CREDIT REQUIREMENTS

THE ODD COUPLE was first present by Saint Subber in the Plymouth Theatre in New York City on March 10, 1965. The performance was directed by Mike Nichols and the set design was by Oliver Smith. The cast was as follows:

SPEED . . . . .Paul Dooley

MURRAY . . . . Nathaniel Frey

ROY . . . . Sidney Armus

VINNIE . . . . John Fiedler

OSCAR MADISON. . . . . .Walter Matthau

FELIX UNGAR . . . . .Art Carney

GWENDOLYN PIGEON . . . . .Carole Shelley

CECILY PIGEON. . . . . Monica Evans

CHARACTERS

(In Order of Their Appearance:)

SPEED

MURRAY

ROY

VINNIE

OSCAR MADISON

FELIX UNGAR

GWENDOLYN PIGEON

CECILY PIGEON

SETTING

An apartment on Riverside Drive. New York City.

TIME

ACT I

A hot summer night.

ACT II

Scene 1: Two weeks later. About 11 p.m.
Scene 2: A few days later. About 8 p.m.

ACT III

The next evening. About 7:30 p.m.

ACT I

(TIME: A warm summer night.)

(SCENE: The apartment of **OSCAR MADISON**'s. *This is one of those large eight-room affairs on Riverside Drive in the upper eighties. The building is about 35 years old and still has vestiges of its glorious past. High ceilings, walk-in closets and thick walls. We are in the living room with doors leading off to kitchen, bedrooms, and a bathroom, and a hallway to other bedrooms. Although the furnishings have been chosen with extreme good taste, the room itself, without the touch and care of a woman these past few months, is now a study in slovenliness. Dirty dishes, discarded clothes, old newspapers, empty bottles, glasses filled and unfilled, opened and unopened laundry packages, mail and disarrayed furniture abound. The only cheerful note left in this room is the lovely view of the New Jersey Palisades through its twelfth floor window. Three months ago, this was a lovely apartment.)*

(AT RISE: The room is filled with smoke. A poker game is in progress. There are six chairs around the table but only four men are sitting. They are simply, **MURRAY, ROY, SPEED** *and* **VINNIE**. **VINNIE**, *with the largest stack of chips in front of him, is nervously tapping his foot and keeps checking his watch.* **ROY** *is watching* **SPEED** *and* **SPEED** *is glaring at* **MURRAY** *with incredulity and utter fascination.* **MURRAY** *is the dealer. He slowly and methodically tries to shuffle. It is a ponderous*

7

and painful business. **SPEED** *shakes his head in disbelief. This is all done wordlessly.)*

SPEED. *(Cups his chin in his hand and looks at* **MURRAY**.*)* …Tell me, Mr. Maverick, is this your first time on the riverboat?

MURRAY. *(With utter disregard.)* You don't like it, get a machine. *(He continues to deal slowly.)*

ROY. Geez, it stinks in here.

VINNIE. *(Looks at his watch.)* What time is it?

SPEED. Again what time is it?

VINNIE. *(Whiny.)* My watch is slow. I'd like to know what time it is.

SPEED. *(Glares at him.)* You're winning ninety-five dollars, that's what time it is… Where the hell are you running?

VINNIE. I'm not running anywhere. I just asked what time it was. Who said anything about running?

ROY. *(Looks at his watch.)* It's ten-thirty.

(Pause. **MURRAY** *continues to shuffle.)*

VINNIE. *(Pause.)* I got to leave by twelve.

SPEED. *(Looks up in despair.)* Oh, Christ!

VINNIE. I told you that when I sat down. I got to leave by twelve. Murray, didn't I say that when I sat down? I said I got to leave by twelve.

SPEED. All right, don't talk to him. He's dealing. *(To* **MURRAY**.*)* Murray, you wanna rest for a while? Go lie down, sweetheart.

MURRAY. You want speed or accuracy, make up your mind. *(He begins to deal slowly.)*

*(***SPEED** *puffs on his cigar angrily.)*

ROY. Hey, you want to do me a really big favor? Smoke towards New Jersey.

*(***SPEED** *blows smoke at* **ROY**.*)*

MURRAY. No kidding, I'm really worried about Felix. *(Points to empty chair.)* He's never been this late before. Maybe somebody should call. *(Yells offstage.)* Hey, Oscar, why don't you call Felix?

ROY. *(Waves hand through smoke.)* Listen, why don't we chip in three dollars apiece and buy another window. How the hell can you breathe in here?

MURRAY. How many cards you got, four?

SPEED. Yes, Murray, we all have four cards. When you give us one more, we'll all have five. If you were to give us two more, we'd have six. Understand how it works now?

ROY. *(Yells offstage.)* Hey, Oscar, what do you say? In or out?

(From offstage we hear OSCAR's voice.)

OSCAR. *(Offstage.)* Out, pussycat, out!

(SPEED opens, and the others bet.)

VINNIE. I told my wife I'd be home by one the latest. We're making an eight o'clock plane to Florida. I told you that when I sat down.

SPEED. Don't cry, Vinnie. You're forty-two years old. It's embarrassing. Give me two... *(Discards.)*

ROY. Why doesn't he fix the air-conditioner? It's ninety-eight degrees and it sits there sweating like everyone else. I'm out. *(Goes to window and looks out.)*

MURRAY. Who goes to Florida in July?

VINNIE. It's off season. There's no crowds and you get the best room for one-tenth the price. No cards...

SPEED. Some vacation. Six cheap people in an empty hotel.

MURRAY. Dealer takes four... Hey, you think maybe Felix is sick? *(He points to empty chair.)* I mean he's never been this late before.

ROY. *(Takes laundry bag from armchair and sits.)* You know it's the same garbage from last week's game. I'm beginning to recognize things.

MURRAY. *(Throwing cards down.)* I'm out...

SPEED. *(Showing hand.)* Two kings...

VINNIE. Straight... *(Shows hand and takes in pot.)*

MURRAY. Hey, maybe he's in his office locked in the john again. Did you know Felix was once locked in the john overnight? He wrote out his entire will on a half a roll of toilet paper! …Heee, what a nut!

>   (**VINNIE** *is playing with his chips.*)

SPEED. (*Glares at him as he shuffles cards.*) Don't play with your chips. I'm asking you nice, don't play with your chips.

VINNIE. (*To* **SPEED**.) I'm not playing. I'm counting. Leave me alone. What are you picking on me for? How much do you think I'm winning? Fifteen dollars!

SPEED. *Fifteen dollars?* You dropped more than that in your cuffs! (**SPEED** *deals a game of draw poker.*)

MURRAY. (*Yells offstage.*) Hey, Oscar, what do you say?

OSCAR. (*Enters carrying a tray with beer, sandwiches, can of peanuts, and opened bags of pretzels and Fritos.*) I'm in! I'm in! Go ahead. Deal!

>   (**OSCAR MADISON** *is 43. He is a pleasant, appealing man. He seems to enjoy life to the fullest. He enjoys his weekly poker game, his friends, his excessive drinking and his cigars. He is also one of those lucky creatures in life who even enjoys his work, a sportswriter for the New York Post. His carefree attitude is evident in the sloppiness of his household but it seems to bother others more than it does* **OSCAR**. *This is all not to say that* **OSCAR** *is without cares or worries. He just doesn't seem to have any.*)

VINNIE. Aren't you going to look at your cards?

OSCAR. (*Sets tray on side chair.*) What for? I'm gonna bluff anyway. (*Opens bottle of Coke.*) Who gets the Coke?

MURRAY. I get a Coke.

OSCAR. My friend Murray, the policeman, gets a warm Coke. (*He gives him the bottle.*)

ROY. (*Opens the betting.*) You still didn't fix the refrigerator? It's been two weeks now. No wonder it stinks in here.

OSCAR. *(Picking up his cards.)* Temper, temper. If I wanted nagging I'd go back with my wife… *(Throws them down.)* I'm out… Who wants food?

MURRAY. What have you got?

OSCAR. *(Looks under bread.)* I got brown sandwiches and green sandwiches… Well, what do you say?

MURRAY. What's the green?

OSCAR. It's either very new cheese or very old meat.

MURRAY. I'll take the brown.

> *(OSCAR gives MURRAY a sandwich.)*

ROY. *(Glares at MURRAY.)* Are you crazy? You're not going to eat that, are you?

MURRAY. I'm hungry.

ROY. His refrigerator's been broken for two weeks. I saw milk standing in there that wasn't even in the bottle.

OSCAR. *(To ROY.)* What are you, some kind of a health nut? Eat, Murray, eat!

ROY. I've got six cards…

SPEED. That figures… I've got three aces. Misdeal.

> *(All throw their cards in. SPEED begins to shuffle.)*

VINNIE. You know who makes very good sandwiches? Felix. Did you ever taste his cream cheese and pimento on date nut bread?

SPEED. *(To VINNIE.)* All right, make up your mind, poker or menus.

> *(OSCAR opens a can of beer, which sprays in a geyser over all players and table. There is a hubbub as they all yell at OSCAR. He hands ROY the overflowing can, and pushes the puddle of beer under the chair. The Players start to go back to the game only to be sprayed by the beer again as OSCAR opens another can. There is another outraged cry as they try to stop OSCAR and mop up the beer on the table with a towel which is hanging on the standing lamp. OSCAR, undisturbed, gives*

*them the beer and the bags of refreshments, and
they finally sit back in their chairs.* **OSCAR** *wipes
his hands on the sleeve of* **ROY**'s *jacket which is
hanging on the back of the chair.)*

SPEED. Hey, Vinnie, tell Oscar what time you're leaving.

VINNIE. *(Like a trained dog.)* Twelve o'clock.

SPEED. *(To others.)* You hear? We got ten minutes before
the next announcement. All right, this game is five-
card stud... *(Deals, and ad libs calling cards, ending with*
MURRAY's *card.)* And a bullet for the policeman... All
right, Murray, it's your bet. *(No answer.)* Do something,
huh?

OSCAR. *(Getting drink at bar.)* Don't yell at my friend Murray.

MURRAY. *(Throwing in coin.)* I'm in for a quarter.

OSCAR. *(Proudly looks in* **MURRAY**'s *eyes.)* Beautiful, baby,
beautiful. *(Sits down and begins to open can of peanuts.)*

ROY. Hey, Oscar, let's make a rule. Every six months you
have to buy fresh potato chips. How can you live like
this? Don't you have a maid?

OSCAR. *(Shakes head.)* She quit after my wife and kids left.
The work got to be too much for her... *(Looks on table.)*
The pot's shy. Who didn't put in a quarter?

MURRAY. *(To* **OSCAR.***)* You didn't.

OSCAR. *(Puts in money.)* You got a big mouth, Murray. Just
for that, lend me twenty dollars.

　　　　*(**SPEED** deals another round.)*

MURRAY. I just loaned you twenty dollars ten minutes ago.

　　　　(All join in a round of betting.)

OSCAR. You loaned me *ten* dollars *twenty* minutes ago.
Learn to count, pussy cat.

MURRAY. Learn to play poker, chicken licken! ...Borrow
from somebody else. I keep winning my own money
back.

ROY. *(To* **OSCAR.***)* You owe everybody in the game. If you
don't have it, you shouldn't play.

OSCAR. ...All right, I'm through being the nice one. You owe me six dollars apiece for the buffet.

SPEED. *(Dealing another round of cards.) Buffet?* Hot beer and two sandwiches left over from when you went to high school?

OSCAR. What do you want at a poker game, a tomato surprise? ...Murray, lend me twenty dollars or I'll call your wife and tell her you're in Central Park wearing a dress.

MURRAY. You want money, ask Felix.

OSCAR. He's not here.

MURRAY. Neither am I.

ROY. *(Gives him money.)* All right, here. You're on the books for another twenty.

OSCAR. How many times are you gonna keep saying it? *(Takes money.)*

MURRAY. When are you gonna call Felix?

OSCAR. When are we gonna play poker?

MURRAY. Aren't you even worried? It's the first game he's missed in over two years.

OSCAR. The record is fifteen years set by Lou Gehrig in 1939! ...I'll call! I'll call!

ROY. How can you be so lazy?

(The phone rings.)

OSCAR. *(Throwing cards in.)* Call me irresponsible, I'm funny that way. *(Goes to phone.)*

SPEED. Pair of sixes...

VINNIE. Three deuces...

SPEED. *(Throws up hands in despair.)* This is my last week. I get all the aggravation I need at home.

(OSCAR picks up phone.)

OSCAR. Hello! Oscar the Poker Player!

VINNIE. *(To OSCAR.)* If it's my wife tell her I'm leaving at twelve.

SPEED. *(To VINNIE.)* You look at your watch once more and you get the peanuts in your face... *(To ROY.)* Deal the cards!

> *(The game continues during OSCAR's phone conversation, with ROY dealing a game of stud.)*

OSCAR. *(Into phone.)* Who? ...Who did you want, please? ...Dabby? Dabby who? ...No, there's no Dabby here... Oh, *Daddy! (To others.)* For crissakes, it's my kid. *(Back into phone, he speaks with great love and affection.)* Brucey, hello, baby. Yes, it's Daddy! *(There is a general outburst of ad-libbing from the Poker Players. To others.)* Hey, come on, give me a break, willya? My five-year-old kid is calling from California. It must be costing him a fortune. *(Back into phone.)* How've you been, sweetheart? ... Yes, I finally got your letter. It took three weeks... Yes, but next time you tell Mommy to give you a stamp... I know, but you're not supposed to draw it on... *(Laughs. To others.)* You hear?

SPEED. We hear. We hear. We're all thrilled.

OSCAR. *(Into phone.)* What's that, darling...? What goldfish? ...Oh, in your room! ...Oh, sure. Sure, I'm taking care of them... *(He holds phone over chest.)* Oh, God, I killed my kid's goldfish! *(Back into phone.)* Yes, I feed them every day.

ROY. Murderer!

OSCAR. Mommy wants to speak to me? Right... Take care of yourself, soldier. I love you.

VINNIE. *(Beginning to deal a game of stud.)* Ante a dollar...

SPEED. *(To OSCAR.)* Cost you a dollar to play. You got a dollar?

OSCAR. Not after I get through talking to this lady. *(Into phone. False cheerfulness.)* Hello, Blanche. How are you? ...Err... Yes... I have a pretty good idea why you're calling... I'm a week behind with the check, right? ...*Four* weeks?? That's not possible... Because it's not possible... Blanche, I keep a record of every check and I *know* I'm only *three* weeks behind! ...Blanche, I'm trying the best I can... Blanche, don't threaten me with jail because it's not a threat... With my expenses and my alimony, a prisoner takes home more pay than I do! ...Very nice, in front of the kids... Blanche, don't tell me you're going to have my salary attached, just say goodbye! ...Goodbye! *(He hangs up. To players.)* I'm eight hundred dollars behind in alimony so let's up the stakes... *(Gets drink from poker table.)*

ROY. She can do it, you know.

OSCAR. What?

ROY. Throw you in jail. For non-support of the kids.

OSCAR. Never. If she can't call me once a week to aggravate me, she's not happy. *(Crosses to bar.)*

MURRAY. It doesn't bother you? That you can go to jail? Or that maybe your kids don't have enough clothes or enough to eat?

OSCAR. Murray... *Poland* could live for a year on what my kids leave over for lunch! ...Can we play cards? *(Refills drink.)*

ROY. But that's the point. You shouldn't *be* in this kind of trouble. It's because you don't know how to manage anything. I should know, I'm your accountant.

OSCAR. *(Crossing to table.)* If you're my accountant, how come I need money?

ROY. If you need money, how come you play poker?

OSCAR. Because I need money.

ROY. But you always lose.

OSCAR. That's why I need the money! ...Listen, *I'm* not complaining. *You're* complaining. I get along all right. I'm living.

ROY. Alone? In eight dirty rooms?

OSCAR. If I win tonight, I'll buy a broom.

> (MURRAY *and* SPEED *buy chips from* VINNIE, *and* MURRAY *begins to shuffle the deck for a game of draw.)*

ROY. That's not what you need. What you need is a wife.

OSCAR. How can I afford a wife when I can't afford a broom?

ROY. Then don't play poker.

OSCAR. *(Puts down drink, rushes to* ROY *and they struggle over the bag of potato chips, which rips showering everyone, who all begin to yell at one another.)* Then don't come to my house and eat my potato chips!

MURRAY. What are you yelling about? We're playing a friendly game.

SPEED. Who's *playing?* We've been sitting here talking since eight o'clock.

VINNIE. Since *seven.* That's why I said I was going to quit at *twelve.*

SPEED. How'd you like a stale banana right in the mouth?

MURRAY. *(The peacemaker.)* All right, all right, let's calm down… Take it easy… I'm a cop, you know. I could arrest the whole lousy game. *(Finishes dealing cards.)* Four…

OSCAR. *(Sitting at table.)* My friend Murray the Cop is right. Let's just play cards. And please hold them up, I can't see where I marked them.

MURRAY. You're worse than the kids from the PAL.

OSCAR. But you still love me, Roy, sweety, right?

ROY. *(Petulant.)* Yeah yeah.

OSCAR. That's not good enough. Come on, say it. In front of the whole poker game. "I love you, Oscar Madison."

ROY. You don't take any of this seriously, do you? You owe money to your wife, your government, your friends…

OSCAR. *(Throws cards down.)* What do you want me to do, Roy, jump in the garbage disposal and grind myself to death? *(The phone rings. He goes to answer it.)* Life goes on even for those of us who are divorced, broke and sloppy. *(Into phone.)* Hello? Divorced, Broke and Sloppy. Oh, hello, sweetheart. *(He becomes very seductive and pulls phone to side and talks low, but still audibly to others, who turn and listen.)* I told you not to call me during the game… I can't talk to you now… You *know* I do, darling… All right, just a minute. *(He turns.)* Murray, it's your wife. *(Puts phone on table and sits on sofa.)*

MURRAY. *(Nods disgustedly as he crosses to phone.)* I wish you *were* having an affair with her… Then she wouldn't bother *me* all the time. *(Picks up phone.)* Hello, Mimi, what's wrong?

>   *(SPEED gets up, stretches, and goes into bathroom.)*

OSCAR. *(Woman's voice, imitating Mimi.)* What time are you coming home? *(Then imitating* MURRAY.*)* I don't know, about twelve, twelve-thirty.

MURRAY. *(Into phone.)* I don't know, about twelve, twelve-thirty! *(ROY gets up and stretches.)* Why, what did you want, Mimi? …"A corned beef sandwich and a strawberry malted!"

OSCAR. Is she pregnant again?

MURRAY. *(Holds phone over chest.)* No, just fat!

>   *(There is the sound of a toilet flushing, and after*
>   SPEED *comes out of the bathroom,* VINNIE *goes in.*
>   *Into phone again.)*

What? …How could you hear that, I had the phone over my chest? …Who? …Felix? …No, he didn't show up tonight… What's wrong? …You're kidding! …How should I know? …All right, all right, goodbye…

>   *(The toilet flushes again, and after* VINNIE *comes*
>   *out of the bathroom,* ROY *goes in.)*

Goodbye, Mimi… Goodbye. *(He hangs up. To others.)* Well, what did I tell you? I knew it!

ROY. What's the matter?

MURRAY. *(Pacing above the couch.)* Felix is missing!

OSCAR. Who?

MURRAY. Felix! Felix Ungar! The man who sits in that chair every week and cleans ashtrays. I told you something was up.

SPEED. *(At the table.)* What do you mean, missing?

MURRAY. He didn't show up for work today. He didn't come home tonight. No one knows where he is. Mimi just spoke to his wife.

VINNIE. *(In his chair at the poker table.)* Felix?

MURRAY. They looked everywhere... I'm telling you he's missing.

OSCAR. Wait a minute. No one is missing for one day.

VINNIE. That's right. You've got to be missing for forty-eight hours before you're missing. The worst he could be is lost.

MURRAY. How could he be lost? He's forty-four years old and lives on West End Avenue. What's the matter with you?

ROY. *(Sitting in armchair.)* Maybe he had an accident.

OSCAR. They would have heard.

ROY. If he's laying in a gutter somewhere? Who would know who he is?

OSCAR. He's got ninety-two credit cards in his wallet. The minute something happens to him, America lights up.

VINNIE. Maybe he went to a movie. You know how long those pictures are today.

SPEED. *(Looks at* VINNIE *contemptuously.)* No wonder you're going to Florida in July! *Dumb dumb dumb!*

ROY. Maybe he was mugged?

OSCAR. For thirty-six hours? How much money could he have on him?

ROY. Maybe they took his clothes. I knew a guy who was mugged in a doctor's office. He had to go home in a nurse's uniform.

(OSCAR *throws a pillow from the couch at* ROY.)

SPEED. Murray, you're a cop. What do you think?

MURRAY. I think it's something real bad.

SPEED. How do you know?

MURRAY. I can feel it in my bones.

SPEED. *(To others.)* You hear? Bulldog Drummond.

ROY. Maybe he's drunk. Does he drink?

OSCAR. Felix? On New Year's Eve he has Pepto Bismal... What are we guessing? I'll call his wife. *(He picks up phone.)*

SPEED. Wait a minute! Don't start anything yet. Just 'cause we don't know where he is doesn't mean *somebody else* doesn't... Does he have a girl?

VINNIE. A what?

SPEED. A girl? You know. Like when you're through work early.

MURRAY. Felix? Playing around? Are you crazy? He wears a vest and galoshes.

SPEED. *(Gets up and moves towards MURRAY.)* You mean you automatically know who has and who hasn't got a girl on the side?

MURRAY. *(Moves to SPEED.)* Yes, I automatically know.

SPEED. All right, you're so smart. Have *I* got a girl?

MURRAY. No, you haven't got a girl. What you've got is what *I've* got. What you *wish* you got and what you *got* is a whole different civilization! ...Oscar maybe has a girl on the side.

SPEED. That's different. He's divorced. That's not on the *side*. That's in the *middle*. (Moves to table.)

OSCAR. *(To them both as he starts to dial.)* You through? 'Cause one of our poker players is missing. I'd like to find out about him.

VINNIE. I thought he looked edgy the last couple of weeks. *(To SPEED.)* Didn't you think he looked edgy?

SPEED. No. As a matter of fact, I thought *you* looked edgy. *(Moves down right.)*

OSCAR. *(Into phone.)* Hello? ...Frances? ...Oscar. I just heard.

ROY. Tell her not to worry. She's probably hysterical.

MURRAY. Yeah, you know women. *(Sits down on couch.)*

OSCAR. *(Into phone.)* Listen, Frances, the most important thing is not to worry... Oh! *(To others.)* She's not worried.

MURRAY. Sure.

OSCAR. *(Into phone.)* Frances, do you have *any* idea where he could be? ...He what? ...You're kidding? ...Why? ...No, I didn't know... Gee, that's too bad... All right, listen, Frances, you just sit tight and the minute I hear anything I'll let you know... Right... G'bye.

> *(He hangs up. They all look at him expectantly. He gets up wordlessly and crosses to the table, thinking. They all watch him a second, not being able to stand it any longer.)*

MURRAY. Ya gonna tell us or do we hire a private detective?

OSCAR. They broke up!

ROY. Who?

OSCAR. Felix and Frances! They broke up! The entire marriage is through.

VINNIE. You're kidding?

ROY. I don't believe it.

SPEED. After twelve years?

> *(OSCAR sits down at the table.)*

VINNIE. They were such a happy couple.

MURRAY. Twelve years doesn't mean you're a *happy* couple. It just means you're a *long* couple.

SPEED. Go figure it. Felix and Frances.

ROY. What are you surprised at? He used to sit there every Friday night and tell us how they were fighting.

SPEED. I know. But who believes Felix?

VINNIE. What happened?

OSCAR. She wants out, that's all.

MURRAY. He'll go to pieces. I know Felix. He's going to try something crazy.

SPEED. That's all he ever used to talk about. "My beautiful wife. My wonderful wife." What happened?

OSCAR. His beautiful, wonderful wife can't stand him, that's what happened.

MURRAY. He'll kill himself. You hear what I'm saying? He's going to go out and try to kill himself.

SPEED. *(To MURRAY.)* Will you shut up, Murray? Stop being a cop for two minutes. *(To OSCAR.)* Where'd he go, Oscar?

OSCAR. He went out to kill himself.

MURRAY. What did I tell you?

ROY. *(To OSCAR.)* Are you serious?

OSCAR. That's what she said. He was going out to kill himself. He didn't want to do it at home 'cause the kids were sleeping.

VINNIE. Why?

OSCAR. Why? Because that's Felix, that's why. *(Goes to bar and refills his drink.)* You know what he's like. He sleeps on the window sill. "Love me or I'll jump" ... 'Cause he's a nut, that's why.

MURRAY. That's right. Remember he tried something like that in the army? She wanted to break off the engagement so he started cleaning guns in his mouth.

SPEED. I don't believe it. Talk! That's all Felix is, talk.

VINNIE. *(Worried.)* But is that what he said? In those words? "I'm going to kill myself"?

OSCAR. *(Pacing about the table.)* I don't know in what words. She didn't read it to me.

ROY. You mean he left her a note?

OSCAR. No, he sent a telegram.

MURRAY. A *suicide telegram?* ...Who sends a *suicide telegram?*

OSCAR. Felix, the nut, that's who! ...Can you imagine getting a thing like that? She even has to tip the kid a quarter.

ROY. I don't get it. If he wants to kill himself, why does he send a telegram?

OSCAR. Don't you see how his mind works? If he sends a note, she might not get it 'til Monday and he'd have no excuse for not being dead. This way, for a dollar ten, he's got a chance to be saved.

VINNIE. You mean he really doesn't want to kill himself? He just wants sympathy.

OSCAR. What *he'd* really like is to go to the funeral and sit in the back. He'd be the biggest cryer there.

MURRAY. He's right.

OSCAR. Sure I'm right...

MURRAY. We get these cases every day. All they want is attention. We got a guy who calls us every Saturday afternoon from the George Washington Bridge.

ROY. I don't know. You never can tell what a guy'll do when he's hysterical.

MURRAY. Nahhh. Nine out of ten times they don't jump.

ROY. What about the tenth time?

MURRAY. They jump. He's right. There's a possibility.

OSCAR. Not with Felix. I know him. He's too nervous to kill himself. He wears his seat belt in a drive-in movie.

VINNIE. Isn't there someplace we could look for him?

SPEED. Where? Where would you look? Who knows *where* he is?

(The doorbell rings. They all look at OSCAR.)

OSCAR. Of course! ...If you're going to kill yourself, where's the safest place to do it? ...With your friends!

(VINNIE starts for door.)

MURRAY. *(Stopping him.)* Wait a minute! The guy may be hysterical. Let's play it nice and easy. If *we're* calm, maybe *he'll* be calm.

ROY. *(Getting up and joining them.)* That's right. That's how they do it with those guys out on the ledge. You talk nice and soft.

(SPEED rushes over to them, and joins in the frenzied discussion.)

VINNIE. What'll we say to him?

MURRAY. We don't say nothin'. Like we never heard a thing.

OSCAR. *(Trying to get their attention.)* You through with this discussion? Because he already could have hung himself out in the hall. *(To VINNIE.)* Vinnie, open the door!

MURRAY. Remember! Like we don't know nothin'.

> *(All rush back to their seats and grab up cards, which they concentrate on with the greatest intensity. VINNIE opens the door. FELIX UNGAR is there. About 44. His clothes are rumpled as if he had slept in them, and he needs a shave. Although he tries to act matter-of-fact, there is an air of great tension and nervousness about him.)*

FELIX. *(Softly.)* Hi, Vin!

> *(VINNIE quickly goes back to his seat and studies his cards. FELIX has his hands in his pockets, trying to be very nonchalant. Controlled calm.)*

Hi, fellas.

> *(They all mumble hello, but do not look at him. He puts his coat over the railing and crosses to the table.)*

How's the game going?

> *(They all mumble appropriate remarks, and continue staring at their cards.)*

Good! …Good! …Sorry I'm late.

> *(FELIX looks a little disappointed that no one asks "What?" …He starts to pick up a sandwich, changes his mind, and makes a gesture of distaste. He vaguely looks around.)*

Any Coke left?

OSCAR. *(Looking up from his cards.)* Coke? …Gee, I don't think so… I got a Seven Up!

FELIX. *(Bravely.)* No… I felt like a Coke. I just don't feel like Seven Up…tonight! *(Stands watching the game.)*

OSCAR. What's the bet?

SPEED. You bet a quarter…it's up to Murray… Murray, what do you say? (**MURRAY** *is staring at* **FELIX**.) Murray! …Murray!

ROY. *(To* **VINNIE**.*)* Tap his shoulder.

VINNIE. *(Taps* **MURRAY**'s *shoulder.)* Murray!

MURRAY. *(Startled.)* What? What?

SPEED. It's up to you.

MURRAY. Why is it always up to me?

SPEED. It's not always up to you. It's up to you now. What do you do?

MURRAY. I'm in. I'm in. *(He throws in quarter.)*

FELIX. *(Moves to bookcase.)* Anyone call about me?

OSCAR. Er…not that I can remember. *(To others.)* Did anyone call for Felix? *(They all shrug and ad-lib "No.")* Why? …Were you expecting a call?

FELIX. *(Looking at books on shelf.)* No! …No! …Just asking. *(He opens book and examines it.)*

ROY. Er… I'll see his bet and raise it a dollar.

FELIX. *(Without looking up from book.)* I just thought someone might have called.

SPEED. It costs me a dollar and a quarter to play, right?

OSCAR. Right!

FELIX. *(Still looking at book…sing-song.)* But…if no one called, no one called. *(Slams book shut and puts it back. All jump at the noise.)*

SPEED. *(Getting nervous.)* What does it cost me to play again?

MURRAY. *(Angry.)* A dollar and a quarter! *A dollar and a quarter!* Pay attention, for crise sakes!

ROY. All right, take it easy. Take it easy.

OSCAR. Let's calm down, everyone, heh?

MURRAY. I'm sorry. I can't help it. *(Points to* **SPEED**.*)* He makes me nervous.

SPEED. I make *you* nervous. You make *me* nervous. You make *everyone* nervous.

MURRAY. *(Sarcastic.)* I'm sorry. Forgive me. I'll kill myself.

OSCAR. Murray! *(He motions with his head to* **FELIX.***)*

MURRAY. *(Realizes his error.)* Oh! …Sorry.

> *(***SPEED** *glares at him. They all sit in silence a moment, until* **VINNIE** *catches sight of* **FELIX** *who is now staring out upstage window. He quickly calls the others' attention to* **FELIX.***)*

FELIX. *(Looking back at them from the window.)* Gee, it's a pretty view from here… What is it, twelve floors?

OSCAR. *(Quickly crossing to the window and closing it.)* No. It's only eleven. That's all. Eleven. It says twelve but it's really only eleven. *(He then turns and closes the other window as* **FELIX** *watches him.* **OSCAR** *shivers slightly.)* Chilly in here. *(To others.)* Isn't it chilly in here? *(Crosses back to table.)*

ROY. Yeah, that's much better.

OSCAR. *(To* **FELIX.***)* Want to sit down and play? It's still early.

VINNIE. Sure. We're in no rush. We'll be here 'til three, four in the morning.

FELIX. *(Shrugs.)* I don't know… I just don't feel much like playing now.

OSCAR. *(Sitting at table.)* Oh! …Well…what *do* you feel like doing?

FELIX. *(Shrugs.)* I'll find something… *(Starts to walk toward other room.)* Don't worry about me…

OSCAR. Where are you going?

FELIX. *(Stops in the doorway. He looks at others who are all staring at him.)* To the john.

OSCAR. *(Looks at others worried, then at* **FELIX.***)* Alone?

FELIX. *(Nods.)* I always go alone! Why?

OSCAR. *(Shrugs.)* No reason! …You gonna be in there long?

FELIX. *(Shrugs, then says meaningfully, like the martyr.)* As long as it takes.

> *(Then he goes into the bathroom and slams the door shut behind him. Immediately they all jump*

up and crowd about the bathroom door, whispering in frenzied anxiety.)

MURRAY. Are you crazy? Letting him go to the john alone?

OSCAR. What did you want me to do?

ROY. Stop him! Go in with him!

OSCAR. Suppose he just has to go to the john?

MURRAY. Supposing he does? He's better off being *embarrassed* than dead!

OSCAR. How's he going to kill himself in the john?

SPEED. What do you mean, how? Razor blades, pills. Anything that's in there.

OSCAR. That's the *kids'* bathroom. The worst he could do is brush his teeth to death.

ROY. He could jump.

VINNIE. That's right. Isn't there a window in there?

OSCAR. It's only six inches wide.

MURRAY. He could break the glass. He could cut his wrists.

OSCAR. He could also flush himself into the East River. I'm telling you he's not going to try anything! *(Moves to table.)*

ROY. *(Goes to doorway.)* Shhh! Listen! He's crying… *(There is a pause as all listen as FELIX sobs.)* You hear that. He's crying.

MURRAY. Isn't that terrible? …For God's sakes, Oscar, do something! Say something!

OSCAR. What? What do you say to a man who's crying in your bathroom?

(There is the sound of the toilet flushing and ROY makes a mad dash back to his chair.)

ROY. He's coming!

(They all scramble back to their places. MURRAY gets mixed up with VINNIE and they quickly straighten it out. FELIX comes back into room. But he seems calm and collected with no evident signs of having cried.)

FELIX. I guess I'll be running along.

(He starts for the door. **OSCAR** *jumps up. So do others.)*

OSCAR. Felix, wait a second.

FELIX. No! No! I can't talk to you. I can't talk to anyone.

(They all try to grab him, stopping him near the stairs.)

MURRAY. Felix, please. We're your friends. Don't run out like this.

*(***FELIX*** *struggles to pull away.)*

OSCAR. Felix, sit down. Just for a minute. Talk to us.

FELIX. There's nothing to talk about. There's nothing to say. It's over. Over. Everything is over. Let me go!

(He breaks away from them and dashes into the stage right bedroom. They start to chase him and he dodges from the bedroom through the adjoining door into the bathroom.)

ROY. Stop him! Grab him!

FELIX. *(Looking for an exit.)* Let me out! I've got to get out of here!

OSCAR. Felix, you're hysterical.

FELIX. Please let me out of here!

MURRAY. The john! Don't let him get in the john!

FELIX. *(Comes out of the bathroom into the room with ***ROY*** hanging onto him, and the others trailing behind.)* Leave me alone. Why doesn't everyone leave me alone?

OSCAR. All right, Felix, I'm warning you... Now cut it out! *(Throws half-filled glass of water, which he has picked up from the bookcase, into ***FELIX***'s face.)*

FELIX. It's *my* problem. I'll work it out. Leave me alone... Ohh, my stomach. *(He collapses in ***ROY***'s arms.)*

MURRAY. What's the matter with your stomach?

VINNIE. He looks sick. Look at his face.

(All try to hold him as they lead him over to the couch.)

FELIX. I'm not sick. I'm all right. I didn't take anything, I swear... Ohh, my stomach.

OSCAR. What do you mean you didn't take anything? What did you take?

FELIX. *(Sitting on couch.)* Nothing! Nothing! I didn't take anything... Don't tell Frances what I did, please! ...Oohh, my stomach.

MURRAY. He took something! I'm telling you he took something.

OSCAR. What, Felix? *What??*

FELIX. Nothing! I didn't take anything.

OSCAR. Pills? Did you take pills?

FELIX. No! No!

OSCAR. *(Grabbing* **FELIX.***)* Don't lie to me, Felix. Did you take pills?

FELIX. No, I didn't. I didn't take anything.

MURRAY. Thank God, he didn't take pills.

(All relax and take a breath of relief.)

FELIX. Just a few, that's all.

(All react in alarm and concern over pills.)

OSCAR. He took pills.

MURRAY. How many pills?

OSCAR. What kind of pills?

FELIX. I don't know what kind. Little green ones. I just grabbed anything out of her medicine cabinet... I must have been crazy.

OSCAR. Didn't you look? Didn't you see what kind?

FELIX. I couldn't see. The light's broken. Don't call Frances. Don't tell her. I'm so ashamed. So ashamed.

OSCAR. Felix, how-many-pills-did-you-take?

FELIX. I don't know. I can't remember.

OSCAR. I'm calling Frances.

FELIX. *(Grabs him.)* No! Don't call her. Don't call her. If she hears I took a whole bottle of pills...

MURRAY. *A whole bottle? A whole bottle of pills? (He turns to* **VINNIE.**) My God, call an ambulance!

(**VINNIE** *runs to the front door.*)

OSCAR. *(To* **MURRAY.**) You don't even know what *kind!*

MURRAY. What's the difference? He took-a-whole-bottle!

OSCAR. Maybe they were vitamins. He could be the healthiest one in the room! ...Take it easy, will you?

FELIX. Don't call Frances. Promise me you won't call Frances.

MURRAY. Open his collar. Open the window. Give him some air.

SPEED. Walk him around. Don't let him go to sleep.

(**SPEED** *and* **MURRAY** *pick* **FELIX** *up and walk him around, while* **ROY** *rubs his wrists.*)

ROY. Rub his wrists. Keep his circulation going.

VINNIE. *(Running to bathroom to get a compress.)* A cold compress. Put a cold compress on his neck.

(*They sit* **FELIX** *in the armchair, still chattering in alarm.*)

OSCAR. One doctor at a time, heh? All the interns shut the hell up!

FELIX. I'm all right. I'll be all right... *(To* **OSCAR** *urgently.*) You didn't call Frances, did you?

MURRAY. *(To others.)* You just gonna stand here? No one's gonna do anything? I'm calling a doctor. *(Crosses to phone.)*

FELIX. No! No doctor.

MURRAY. You *gotta* have a doctor.

FELIX. I don't need a doctor.

MURRAY. You gotta get the pills out.

FELIX. I got them out. I threw up before! ...

(*Sits back weakly.* **MURRAY** *hangs up the phone.*)

Don't you have a root beer or a ginger ale?

(**VINNIE** *gives compress to* **SPEED.**)

ROY. *(To* **VINNIE.***)* Get him a drink.

OSCAR. *(Glares angrily at* **FELIX.***)* He threw them up!

VINNIE. Which would you rather have, Felix, the root beer or the ginger ale?

SPEED. *(To* **VINNIE.***)* Get him the drink! Just get him the drink.

> *(***VINNIE*** *runs into the kitchen as* **SPEED** *puts the compress on* **FELIX***'s head.)*

FELIX. Twelve years. Twelve years we were married. Did you know we were married twelve years, Roy?

ROY. *(Comforting him.)* Yes, Felix. I knew.

FELIX. *(Great emotion in his voice.)* And now it's over. Like that it's over. That's hysterical, isn't it?

SPEED. Maybe it was just a fight. You've had fights before, Felix.

FELIX. No, it's over. She's getting a lawyer tomorrow... *My* cousin... She's using *my* cousin! ... *(He sobs.)* Whom am *I* going to get? ...

> *(***VINNIE*** *comes out of kitchen with glass of root beer.)*

MURRAY. *(Patting his shoulder.)* It's okay, Felix. Come on. Take it easy.

VINNIE. *(Gives glass to* **FELIX.***)* Here's the root beer.

FELIX. I'm all right. Honestly... I'm just crying.
(He puts his head down. They all look at him helplessly.)

MURRAY. All right, let's not stand around looking at him. *(Pushes* **SPEED** *and* **VINNIE** *away.)* Let's break it up, heh?

FELIX. Yes, don't stand there looking at me. Please.

OSCAR. *(To others.)* Come on, he's all right. Let's call it a night.

> *(***MURRAY, SPEED*** *and* **ROY** *turn in their chips at the poker table, get their coats and get ready to go.)*

FELIX. I'm so ashamed. Please, fellas, forgive me.

VINNIE. *(Bending to* **FELIX.***)* Oh, Felix, we—we understand.

FELIX. Don't say anything about this to anyone, Vinnie. Will you promise me?

VINNIE. I'm going to Florida tomorrow.

FELIX. Oh, that's nice. Have a good time.

VINNIE. Thanks.

FELIX. *(Turns away and sighs in despair.)* We were going to go to Florida next winter. *(He laughs, but it's a sob.)* Without the kids! ...Now they'll go without me.

> (VINNIE *gets his coat and* OSCAR *ushers them all to the door.)*

MURRAY. *(Stopping at door.)* Maybe one of us should stay?

OSCAR. It's all right, Murray.

MURRAY. Suppose he tries something again?

OSCAR. He won't try anything again.

MURRAY. How do you *know* he won't try anything again?

FELIX. *(Turns to* MURRAY.*)* I won't try anything again. I'm very tired.

OSCAR. *(To* MURRAY.*)* You hear? He's very tired. He had a busy night... Good night, fellows...

> *(All ad-lib goodbyes and leave. The door closes, but opens immediately and* ROY *comes back in.)*

ROY. If anything happens, Oscar, just call me.

> *(He exits, and as door starts to close, it reopens and* SPEED *comes in.)*

SPEED. I'm three blocks away. I could be here in five minutes.

> *(He exits, and as door starts to close it reopens and* VINNIE *comes back in.)*

VINNIE. If you need me I'll be at the Meridian Motel in Miami Beach.

OSCAR. You'll be the first one I'll call, Vinnie.

> (VINNIE *exits. The door closes and then reopens as* MURRAY *comes back.)*

MURRAY. *(To* **OSCAR**.*)* You're sure?

OSCAR. I'm sure.

MURRAY. *(Loud to* **FELIX**, *as he gestures to* **OSCAR** *to come to door.)* Good night, Felix. Try to get a good night's sleep. I guarantee you things are going to look a lot brighter in the morning. *(To* **OSCAR**, *sotto voce.)* Take away his belt and his shoe laces.

> *(He nods and exits.* **OSCAR** *turns and looks at* **FELIX** *sitting in the armchair and slowly moves across the room. There is a moment's silence.)*

OSCAR. *(He looks at* **FELIX** *and sighs.)* Ohh, Felix, Felix, Felix, Felix!

FELIX. *(Sits with his head buried in his hands. He doesn't look up.)* I know, I know, I know, I know! …What am I going to do, Oscar?

OSCAR. You're gonna wash down the pills with some hot, black coffee… *(He starts for kitchen, then stops.)* Do you think I could leave you alone for two minutes?

FELIX. No, I don't think so! …Stay with me, Oscar. Talk to me.

OSCAR. A cup of black coffee. It'll be good for you. Come on in the kitchen. I'll sit on you.

FELIX. Oscar, the terrible thing is, I think I still love her. It's a lousy marriage but I still love her… I didn't want this divorce.

OSCAR. *(Sitting on arm of couch.)* How about some Ovaltine? You like Ovaltine? With a couple of Fig Newtons…or chocolate mallomars?

FELIX. All right, so we didn't get along… But we had two wonderful kids…and a beautiful home… Didn't we, Oscar?

OSCAR. How about vanilla wafers? …Or Vienna Fingers? …I got everything.

FELIX. What more does she want? What does *any* woman want?

OSCAR. I want to know what *you* want. Ovaltine, coffee or tea. Then we'll get to the divorce.

FELIX. It's not fair, dammit! It's just not fair! *(He bangs his fist on the arm of the chair angrily and suddenly winces in great pain and grabs his neck.)* Ohh! Ohh, my neck. My neck!

OSCAR. What? What?

FELIX. *(He is up and paces in pain. He is holding his twisted neck.)* It's a nerve spasm. I get it in the neck. Ohh! Ohh, that hurts.

OSCAR. *(Rushing to help.)* Where? Where does it hurt?

FELIX. *(Stretches out arm like a halfback.)* Don't touch me! Don't touch me!

OSCAR. I just want to see where it hurts.

FELIX. It'll go way. Just let me alone a few minutes… Ohh! …Ohh!

OSCAR. *(Moving to couch.)* Lie down, I'll rub it. It'll ease the pain.

FELIX. *(In wild contortions.)* You don't know how. It's a special way. Only Frances knows how to rub me.

OSCAR. You want me to ask her to come over and rub you?

FELIX. *(Yells.) No!* No! … We're getting divorced. She wouldn't want to rub me anymore… It's tension. I get it from tension. I must be tense.

OSCAR. I wouldn't be surprised. How long does it last?

FELIX. Sometimes a minute, sometimes hours… I once got it while I was driving… I crashed into a liquor store… Ohhh! Ohhh! *(He sits, painfully, on the couch.)*

OSCAR. *(Getting behind him.)* You want to suffer or do you want me to rub your stupid neck? *(He starts to massage it.)*

FELIX. Easy! Easy!

OSCAR. *(Yells.)* Relax… Dammit, relax!

FELIX. *(Yells back.)* Don't yell at me! … *(Then quietly.)* What should I do? Tell me nicely.

OSCAR. *(Rubbing neck.)* Think of warm jello! …

FELIX. Isn't that terrible? I can't do it… I can't relax. I sleep in one position all night… Frances says when I die on my tombstone it's going to say, "Here Stands Felix Ungar." *(He winces.)* Oh! Ohh!

OSCAR. *(Stops rubbing.)* Does that hurt?

FELIX. No, it feels good.

OSCAR. Then say so. You make the same sound for pain or happiness. *(Starts to massage neck again.)*

FELIX. I know. I know… Oscar—I think I'm crazy.

OSCAR. Well, if it'll make you feel any better… I think so, too.

FELIX. I mean it. Why else do I go to pieces like this? Coming up here, scaring you to death. Trying to kill myself. What is that?

OSCAR. That's panic. You're a panicky person. You have a low threshold for composure. *(Stops rubbing.)*

FELIX. Don't stop. It feels good…

OSCAR. If you don't relax I'll break my fingers… *(Touches his hair.)* Look at this… The only man in the world with clenched hair…

FELIX. I do terrible things, Oscar. You know I'm a crybaby.

OSCAR. Bend over.

>   *(**FELIX** bends over and **OSCAR** begins to massage his back.)*

FELIX. *(Head down.)* I tell the whole world my problems.

OSCAR. *(Massaging hard.)* Listen, if this hurts just tell me because I don't know what the hell I'm doing.

FELIX. It just isn't nice, Oscar, running up here like this, carrying on like a nut.

OSCAR. *(Finishes massaging.)* How does your neck feel?

FELIX. *(Twists neck.)* Better. Only my back hurts. *(Gets up and paces, rubbing back.)*

OSCAR. What you need is a drink. *(He starts for bar.)*

FELIX. I can't drink. It makes me sick. I tried drinking last night.

OSCAR. *(At bar.)* Where *were* you last night?

FELIX. Nowhere. I just walked.

OSCAR. All night?

FELIX. All night.

OSCAR. In the rain?

FELIX. No. In a hotel. I couldn't sleep. I walked around the room all night… It was over near Times Square. A dirty, depressing room. Then I found myself looking out the window. And suddenly… I began to think about jumping.

OSCAR. *(He has two glasses filled and crosses to* FELIX.*)* What changed your mind?

FELIX. Nothing. I'm still thinking about it.

OSCAR. Drink this. *(He hands him glass, crosses to the couch and sits.)*

FELIX. I don't want to get divorced, Oscar. I don't want to suddenly change my whole life… *(Moves to couch and sits next to* OSCAR.*)* Talk to me, Oscar. What am I going to do? …What am I going to do?

OSCAR. You're going to pull yourself together. And then you're going to drink that Scotch and then you and I are going to figure out a whole new life for you.

FELIX. Without Frances? Without the kids?

OSCAR. It's been done before.

FELIX. *(Paces right.)* You don't understand, Oscar. I'm nothing without them. I'm *nothing!*

OSCAR. What do you mean, nothing? You're *something!*

(FELIX *sits in armchair.*)

A person! You're flesh and blood and bones and hair and nails and ears. You're not a fish. You're not a buffalo. You're *you!* …You walk and talk and cry and complain and eat little green pills and send suicide telegrams. No one else does that, Felix. I'm telling you, *you're-the-only-one-of-its-kind-in-the-world! (Goes to bar.)* Now drink that.

FELIX. Oscar, you've been through it yourself. What did you do? How did you get through those first few nights?

OSCAR. *(Pours drink.)* I did exactly what you're doing.

FELIX. Getting hysterical!

OSCAR. No, drinking! *Drinking! (Comes back to couch with bottle. Sits.)* I drank for four days and four nights. And then I fell through a window. I was bleeding but I was forgetting. *(He drinks again.)*

FELIX. How can you forget your kids? How can you wipe out twelve years of marriage?

OSCAR. You can't. When you walk into eight empty rooms every night it hits you in the face like a wet glove. But those are the facts, Felix. You've got to face it. You can't spend the rest of your life crying. It annoys people in the movies! ...Be a good boy and drink your Scotch. *(Stretches out on couch with head near* **FELIX**.*)*

FELIX. I can imagine what Frances must be going through.

OSCAR. What do you mean, what *she's* going through?

FELIX. It's much harder on the woman, Oscar. She's all alone with the kids. Stuck there in the house. She can't get out like me. I mean where is she going to find someone now at her age? With two kids. Where?

OSCAR. I don't know. Maybe someone'll come to the door! ...Felix, there's a hundred thousand divorces a year. There must be *something* nice about it. *(***FELIX** *suddenly puts both his hands over his ears and hums quietly.)* What's the matter now? *(Sits up.)*

FELIX. My ears are closing up. I get it from the sinus. It must be the dust in here. I'm allergic to dust. *(Hums. Then gets up and tries to clear ears by hopping first on one leg then the other as he goes to the window and opens it.)*

OSCAR. *(Jumping up.)* What are you doing?

FELIX. I'm not going to jump. I'm just going to breathe. *(He takes deep breaths.)* I used to drive Frances crazy with my allergies. I'm allergic to perfume. For a while the only thing she could wear was my after shave lotion... I was impossible to live with. It's a wonder she took it this long. *(He suddenly bellows like a moose. He does this strange sound another time.* OSCAR *looks at him dumbfounded.)*

OSCAR. What are you doing?

FELIX. I'm trying to clear my ears. You create a pressure inside and then it opens it up. *(He bellows again.)*

OSCAR. Did it open up?

FELIX. A little bit. *(He rubs neck.)* I think I strained my throat. *(Paces about the room.)*

OSCAR. Felix, why don't you leave yourself alone? Don't tinker.

FELIX. I can't help myself. I drive everyone crazy. A marriage counselor once kicked me out of his office. He wrote on my chart, Lunatic! ...I don't blame her. It's impossible to be married to me.

OSCAR. It takes two to make a rotten marriage. *(Lies back down on couch.)*

FELIX. You don't know what I was like at home. I bought her a book and made her write down every penny we spent. Thirty-eight cents for cigarettes, ten cents for a paper. Everything had to go in the book. And then we had a big fight because I said she forgot to write down how much the book was... Who could live with anyone like that?

OSCAR. An accountant! ...What do I know? We're not perfect. We all have faults.

FELIX. Faults? Heh! ...Faults... We have a maid who comes in to clean three times a week. And on the other days, Frances does the cleaning. And at night, after they've both cleaned up, I go in and clean the whole place again. I can't help it. I like things clean. Blame it on my mother. I was toilet trained at five months old.

OSCAR. How do you remember things like that?

FELIX. *I* loused up the marriage. Nothing was ever right. I used to recook everything. The minute she walked out of the kitchen I would add salt or pepper. It's not that I didn't trust her, it's just that I was a better cook... Well, I cooked myself out of a marriage. *(He bangs his head*

with the palm of his hand three times.) God-damned-idiot!
(Sinks down in armchair.)

OSCAR. Don't do that, you'll get a headache.

FELIX. I can't stand it, Oscar. I hate me. Oh, boy, do I hate
me.

OSCAR. You don't hate you. You love you. You think no one
has problems like you.

FELIX. Don't give me that analyst jazz. I happen to know I
hate my guts.

OSCAR. Come on, Felix, I've never *seen* anyone so in love.

FELIX. *(Hurt.)* I thought you were my friend.

OSCAR. That's why I can talk to you like this. Because I love
you almost as much as *you* do...

FELIX. Then help me.

OSCAR. *(Up on one elbow.)* How can I help you when I can't
help myself? You think *you're* impossible to live with?
Blanche used to say, "What time do you want dinner?"
And I'd say, "I don't know. I'm not hungry." Then at
three o'clock in the morning I'd wake her up and
say, "Now!" ...I've been one of the highest paid sports
writers in the East for the past fourteen years—and we
saved eight and a half dollars—in pennies! I'm never
home, I gamble, I burn cigar holes in the furniture,
drink like a fish and lie to her every chance I get,
and for our tenth wedding anniversary, I took her to
see the New York Rangers-Detroit Red Wings hockey
game, where she got hit with a puck. And I *still* can't
understand why she left me. That's how impossible *I*
am!

FELIX. I'm not like you, Oscar. I couldn't take it living all
alone. I don't know how I'm going to work. They've got
to fire me... How am I going to make a living?

OSCAR. You'll go on street corners and cry. They'll throw
nickels at you! ...You'll work, Felix, you'll work. *(Lies
back down.)*

FELIX. You think I ought to call Frances?

OSCAR. *(About to explode.)* What for? *(Sits up.)*

FELIX. Well…talk it out again.

OSCAR. You've *talked* it all out. There are no words left in your entire marriage. When are you going to face up to it?

FELIX. I can't help it, Oscar, I don't know what to do.

OSCAR. Then listen to me. Tonight you're going to sleep here. And tomorrow you're going to get your clothes and your electric tooth brush and you'll move in with me.

FELIX. No, no. It's your apartment. I'll be in the way.

OSCAR. There's eight rooms. We could go for a year without seeing each other… Don't you understand? I *want* you to move in.

FELIX. Why? I'm a pest.

OSCAR. I *know* you're a pest. You don't have to keep telling me.

FELIX. Then why do you want me to live with you?

OSCAR. Because I can't-stand-living-alone, that's why! …For crying out loud, I'm proposing to you. What do you want, a ring?

FELIX. *(Moves to* OSCAR.*)* Well, Oscar, if you really mean it, there's a lot I can do around here. I'm very handy around the house. I can fix things.

OSCAR. You don't have to fix things.

FELIX. I want to do *something*, Oscar. Let me do something.

OSCAR. *(Nods.)* All right, you can take my wife's initials off the towels. Anything you want.

FELIX. *(Beginning to tidy up.)* I can cook. I'm a terrific cook.

OSCAR. You don't have to cook. I eat cold cuts for breakfast.

FELIX. Two meals a day at home, we'll save a fortune. We've got to pay alimony, you know.

OSCAR. *(Happy to see* FELIX's *new optimism.)* All right, you can cook. *(Throws pillow at him.)*

FELIX. *(Throws pillow back.)* Do you like leg of lamb?

OSCAR. Yes, I like leg of lamb.

FELIX. I'll make it tomorrow night... I'll have to call Frances. She has my big pot.

OSCAR. *Will you forget Frances!* We'll get our own pots. Don't drive me crazy before you move in. *(The phone rings.* **OSCAR** *picks it up quickly.)* Hello? ...Oh, hello, Frances!

FELIX. *(Stops cleaning and starts to wave his arms wildly and whispers screamingly.)* I'm not here! I'm not here! You didn't see me. You don't know where I am. I didn't call. I'm not here. I'm not here.

OSCAR. *(Into phone.)* Yes, he's here.

FELIX. *(Pacing back and forth.)* How does she sound? Is she worried? Is she crying? What is she saying? Does she want to speak to me? I don't want to speak to her.

OSCAR. *(Into phone.)* Yes, he is! ...

FELIX. You can tell her I'm not coming back. I've made up my mind. I've had it there. I've taken just as much as she has. You can tell her for me if she thinks I'm coming back she's got another think coming. Tell her. Tell her.

OSCAR. *(Into phone.)* Yes! ...Yes, he's fine.

FELIX. Don't tell her I'm fine! You heard me carrying on before. What are you telling her that for? I'm not fine.

OSCAR. *(Into phone.)* Yes, I understand, Frances.

FELIX. *(Sits down next to* **OSCAR.***)* Does she want to speak to me? Ask her if she wants to speak to me?

OSCAR. *(Into phone.)* Do you want to speak to him?

FELIX. *(Reaches for phone.)* Give me the phone. I'll speak to her.

OSCAR. *(Into phone.)* Oh. You don't want to speak to him.

FELIX. She doesn't want to speak to me?

OSCAR. *(Into phone.)* Yeah, I see... Right... Well, goodbye. *(He hangs up.)*

FELIX. She didn't want to speak to me?

OSCAR. No!

FELIX. Why did she call?

OSCAR. She wants to know when you're coming over for your clothes... She wants to have the room repainted.

FELIX. Oh!

OSCAR. *(Pats FELIX on shoulder.)* Listen, Felix, it's almost one o'clock. *(Gets up.)*

FELIX. Didn't want to speak to me, huh?

OSCAR. I'm going to bed. Do you want a cup of tea with Fruitanos or Raisonettos?

FELIX. She'll paint it pink. She always wanted it pink.

OSCAR. I'll get you a pair of pajamas. You like stripes, dots, or animals? *(Goes into downstage bedroom.)*

FELIX. She's really heartbroken, isn't she? ...I want to kill myself and she's picking out colors.

OSCAR. *(In bedroom.)* Which bedroom do you want? I'm lousy with bedrooms.

FELIX. *(Up and moves towards bedroom.)* You know, I'm glad. Because she finally made me realize...it's over. It didn't sink in until just this minute.

OSCAR. *(Comes back with pillow, pillowcase, and pajamas.)* Felix, I want you to go to bed.

FELIX. I don't think I believed her until just now. My marriage is *really* over.

OSCAR. Felix, go to bed.

FELIX. Somehow it doesn't seem so bad now. I mean I think I can live with this thing.

OSCAR. Live with it tomorrow. Go to bed tonight.

FELIX. In a little while. I've got to think. I've got to start rearranging my life... Do you have a pencil and paper?

OSCAR. Not in a little while. Now! It's my house, I make up the bedtime. *(Throws pajamas to him.)*

FELIX. Oscar, please... I have to be alone for a few minutes. I've got to get organized. Go on, you go to bed... I'll—I'll clean up. *(Begins picking up debris from floor.)*

OSCAR. *(Putting pillow in pillowcase.)* You don't have to clean up. I pay a dollar fifty an hour to clean up.

FELIX. It's all right, Oscar, I wouldn't be able to sleep with all this dirt around anyway. Go to bed. I'll see you in the morning. *(Puts dishes on tray.)*

OSCAR. You're not going to do anything big, are you, like rolling up the rugs?

FELIX. Ten minutes, that's all I'll be.

OSCAR. You're sure…?

FELIX. *(Smiles.)* I'm sure.

OSCAR. No monkey business?

FELIX. No monkey business… I'll do the dishes and go right to bed.

OSCAR. Yeah… *(Crosses up to his bedroom, throwing pillow into the downstage bedroom as he passes. Closes his bedroom door behind him.)*

FELIX. *(Calls him.)* Oscar! *(OSCAR anxiously comes out of his bedroom and crosses to FELIX.)* I'm going to be all right! …It's going to take me a couple of days…but I'm going to be all right.

OSCAR. *(Smiles.)* Good! Well—good night, Felix.

> *(He turns to go towards bedroom as FELIX begins to plump up pillow from the couch.)*

FELIX. Good night, Frances.

> *(OSCAR stops dead. FELIX, unaware of his error, plumps another pillow as OSCAR turns and stares at FELIX with a troubled, troubled expression.)*
>
> *(Curtain.)*

ACT II

Scene One

(TIME: Two weeks later. About 11:00 p.m.)

(AT RISE: It is late in the evening and the poker game is in session again. **VINNIE, ROY, SPEED, MURRAY** *and* **OSCAR** *are all seated at the table.* **FELIX**'s *chair is empty. There is one major difference between this scene and the opening poker game scene. It is the appearance of the room. It is immaculately clean. No, not clean. Sterile! Spotless! Not a speck of dirt can be seen under the ten coats of Johnson's Glo-Coat that have been applied in the last two weeks. No laundry bags, no dirty dishes, no half-filled glasses. Suddenly* **FELIX** *appears from the kitchen. He carries a tray with glasses and food and napkins. After putting the tray down, he takes the napkins one at a time, flicks them out to full length and hands one to every player. They take them with grumbling and put them on their laps.* **FELIX** *picks up a can of beer and very carefully pours it into a tall glass, measuring it perfectly so that not a drop spills or overflows. With a flourish he puts can down.)*

FELIX. *(Moves to* **MURRAY.**) …An ice-cold glass of beer for Murray.

MURRAY. *(He reaches up for it.)* Thank you, Felix.

FELIX. *(Holds glass back.)* Where's your coaster?

MURRAY. My what?

FELIX. Your coaster. The little round thing that goes under the glass.

MURRAY. *(Looks around on the table.)* I think I bet it.

OSCAR. *(Picks it up and hands it to* **MURRAY.**) I knew I was winning too much. Here!

FELIX. Always try to use your coasters, fellows. *(He picks up another drink from tray.)* Scotch and a little bit of water?

SPEED. *(Raises hand.)* Scotch and a little bit of water. *(Proudly.)* And I have my coaster. *(He holds it up for inspection.)*

FELIX. *(Hands him drink.)* I hate to be a pest, but you know what wet glasses do? *(Goes back to the tray and picks up and wipes a clean ashtray.)*

OSCAR. *(Coldly and deliberately.)* They-leave-little-rings-on-the-table.

FELIX. *(Nods.)* Ruins the finish. Eats right through the polish.

OSCAR. *(To others.)* So let's watch those little rings, huh?

FELIX. *(Takes ashtray and plate with a sandwich from tray and crosses to table.)* And we have a clean ashtray for Roy... *(Handing* **ROY** *ashtray.)* Aaaaand...a sandwich for Vinnie. *(Like a doting headwaitery he skillfully places the sandwich in front of* **VINNIE.**)

VINNIE. *(Looks at* **FELIX,** *then at sandwich.)* Gee, it smells good. What is it?

FELIX. Bacon, lettuce and tomato with mayonnaise on pumpernickel toast.

VINNIE. *(Unbelievingly.)* Where'd you get it?

FELIX. *(Puzzled.)* I made it. In the kitchen.

VINNIE. You mean you put in toast and cooked bacon? Just for me?

OSCAR. If you don't like it, he'll make you a meatloaf. Takes him five minutes.

FELIX. It's no trouble. Honest. I love to cook... Try to eat over the dish. I just vacuumed the rug. *(Goes back to tray, stops.)* Oscar!

OSCAR. *(Quickly.)* Yes, sir?

FELIX. I forgot what you wanted. What did you ask me for?

OSCAR. Two three-and-a-half-minute eggs and some petit fours.

FELIX. *(Points to him.)* A double gin and tonic. I'll be right back... **(FELIX** *starts out, then stops at a little box on the bar.)* Who turned off the Pure-A-Tron?

MURRAY. The what?

FELIX. The Pure-A-Tron! *(He snaps it back on.)* Don't play with this, fellows. I'm trying to get some of the grime out of the air.

> *(He looks at them and shakes his head disapprovingly, and exits. They all sit in silence a few seconds.)*

OSCAR. Murray—I'll give you two hundred dollars for your gun.

SPEED. *(Throws his cards on table and gets up angrily.)* I can't take it anymore. *(Hand on neck.)* I've had it up to here. In the last three hours we played four minutes of poker. I'm not giving up my Friday nights to watch cooking and housekeeping.

ROY. *(Slumped in his chair, head hanging down.)* I can't breathe. *(Points to Pure-A-Tron.)* That lousy machine is sucking everything out of the air.

VINNIE. *(Chewing.)* Gee, this is delicious. Who wants a bite?

MURRAY. Is the toast warm?

VINNIE. Perfect. And not too much mayonnaise. It's really a well-made sandwich.

MURRAY. Cut me off a little piece.

VINNIE. Give me your napkin. I don't want to drop any crumbs.

SPEED. *(Watches them, horrified, as* **VINNIE** *carefully breaks sandwich over* **MURRAY**'s *napkin. Then turns to* **OSCAR**.*)* Are you listening to this? Martha and Gertrude at the Automat. *(Almost crying in despair.)* What the hell happened to our poker game?

ROY. *(Still choking.)* I'm telling you that thing could kill us. They'll find us here in the morning with our tongues on the floor.

SPEED. *(Yells at* **OSCAR.***)* Do something! Get him back in the game.

OSCAR. *(Rises, containing his anger.)* Don't bother me with your petty little problems. You get this one stinkin' night a week. I'm cooped up here with Mary Poppins twenty-four hours a day. *(Moves to window.)*

ROY. It was better before. With the garbage and the smoke, it was better before.

VINNIE. *(To* **MURRAY.***)* Did you notice what he does with the bread?

MURRAY. What?

VINNIE. He cuts off the crusts. That's why the sandwich is so light.

MURRAY. And then he only uses the soft, green part of the lettuce. *(Chewing.)* It's really delicious.

SPEED. *(Reacts in amazement and disgust.)* I'm going out of my mind.

OSCAR. *(Yells towards kitchen.)* Felix! ...Damn it, *FELIX!*

SPEED. *(Takes kitty box from bookcase, puts it on table, and puts money in.)* Forget it. I'm going home.

OSCAR. Sit down!

SPEED. I'll buy a book and I'll start to read again.

OSCAR. Siddown! Will you siddown! *(Yells.)* Felix!

SPEED. Oscar, it's all over. The day his marriage busted up was the end of our poker game. *(Takes his jacket from back of chair and crosses to door.)* If you find some real players next week, call me.

OSCAR. *(Following him.)* You can't run out now. I'm a big loser.

SPEED. *(With door open.)* You got no one to blame but yourself. It's all your fault. You're the one who stopped him from killing himself. *(He exits and slams door.)*

OSCAR. *(Stares at door.)* He's right! ...The man is absolutely right. *(Moves to table.)*

MURRAY. *(To* **VINNIE.**) Are you going to eat that pickle?

VINNIE. I wasn't thinking of it. Why? Do you want it?

MURRAY. Unless you want it. It's your pickle.

VINNIE. No, no. Take it. I don't usually eat pickle.

> *(***VINNIE*** holds plate with pickle out to* **MURRAY.** *****OSCAR*** slaps the plate which sends the pickle flying through the air.)*

OSCAR. Deal the cards!

MURRAY. What did you do that for?

OSCAR. Just deal the cards. You want to play poker, deal the cards. You want to eat, go to Schrafft's. *(To* **VINNIE.**) Keep your sandwich and your pickles to yourself... I'm losing ninety-two dollars and everybody's getting fat! *(He screams.) Felix...*

> *(***FELIX*** appears in the kitchen doorway.)*

FELIX. What?

OSCAR. Close the kitchen and sit down. It's a quarter to twelve. I still got an hour and a half to win this month's alimony.

ROY. *(Sniffs.)* What is that smell? Disinfectant! *(He smells cards.)* It's the cards. *He washed the cards! (Throws down cards, takes jacket from chair and moves above table. Puts money into kitty box.)*

FELIX. *(Comes to table with* **OSCAR**'s *drink, which he puts down, and then sits in his own seat.)* Okay... What's the bet?

OSCAR. *(Hurrying to his seat.)* I can't believe it. We're gonna play cards again. *(He sits.)* It's up to Roy... Roy, baby, what are you gonna do?

ROY. I'm going to get in a cab and go to Central Park. If I don't get some fresh air, you got yourself a dead accountant. *(Moves towards door.)*

OSCAR. *(Follows him.)* What do you mean? It's not even twelve o'clock.

ROY. *(Turns back to* **OSCAR.***)* Look, I've been sitting here breathing lysol and ammonia for four hours! ...Nature didn't intend for poker to be played like that. *(He crosses to door.)* If you wanna have a game next week... *(He points to* **FELIX.***)* either Louis Pasteur cleans up *after* we've gone...or we play in the Hotel Dixie! Good night! *(He goes and slams door.)*

> *(There is a moment's silence.* **OSCAR** *goes back to table and sits.)*

OSCAR. We got just enough for handball!

FELIX. Gee, I'm sorry. Is it my fault?

VINNIE. No, I guess no one feels like playing much lately.

MURRAY. Yeah. I don't know what it is, but something's happening to the old gang. *(Goes to side chair, sits, and puts on shoes.)*

OSCAR. Don't you know what's happening to the old gang? It's breaking up. Everyone's getting divorced... I swear, we used to have better games when we couldn't get out at night.

VINNIE. *(Getting up and putting on jacket.)* Well—I guess I'll be going, too. Bebe and I are driving to Asbury Park for the weekend.

FELIX. Just the two of you, heh? Gee, that's nice! ...You always do things like that together, don't you?

VINNIE. *(Shrugs.)* We have to. I don't know how to drive! ... *(Takes all the money from the kitty box and moves to door.)* You coming, Murray?

MURRAY. *(Gets up, takes jacket and moves towards door.)* Yeah, why not? If I'm not home by one o'clock with a hero sandwich and a frozen éclair, she'll have an all-points out on me... Ahhh, you guys got the life.

FELIX. Who?

MURRAY. *(Turns back.)* Who? ...You! The Marx Brothers! Laugh laugh laugh. What have you got to worry about? ...If you suddenly want to go to the Playboy Club to hunt Bunnies, who's gonna stop you?

FELIX. I don't belong to the Playboy Club.

MURRAY. I know you don't, Felix, it's just a figure of speech... Anyway, it's not such a bad idea. Why don't you join?

FELIX. Why?

MURRAY. *Why?* Because for twenty-five dollars they give you a key—and you walk into Paradise. *My* keys cost thirty cents—and you walk into corned beef and cabbage. *(He winks at him.)* Listen to me. *(Moves to door.)*

FELIX. What are you talking about, Murray? You're a happily married man.

MURRAY. *(Turns back on landing.)* I'm not talking about *my* situation... *(Puts on jacket.)* I'm talking about *yours!* ...Fate has just played a cruel and rotten trick on you... so enjoy it! *(Turns to go, revealing "PAL" letters sewn on back of his jacket.)* C'mon, Vinnie.

  (VINNIE waves goodbye and they both exit.)

FELIX. *(Staring at door.)* That's funny, isn't it, Oscar? ...They think we're happy... They really think we're enjoying this... *(Gets up and begins to straighten up chairs.)* They don't know, Oscar. They don't know what it's like. *(He gives a short, ironic laugh, tucks napkins under arm and starts to pick up dishes from table.)*

OSCAR. I'd be immensely grateful to you, Felix, if you didn't clean up just now.

FELIX. *(Puts dishes on tray.)* It's only a few things... *(He stops and looks back at door.)* I can't get over what Murray just said... You know I think they really envy us. *(Clears more stuff from table.)*

OSCAR. Felix, leave everything alone. I'm not through dirtying up for the night. *(Drops poker chips on floor.)*

FELIX. *(Putting stuff on tray.)* But don't you see the irony of it? ... Don't you see it, Oscar?

OSCAR. *(Sighs heavily.)* Yes, I see it.

FELIX. *(Clearing table.)* No, you don't. I really don't think you do.

OSCAR. Felix, I'm telling you I see the irony of it.

FELIX. *(Pauses.)* Then tell me. What is it? What's the irony?

OSCAR. *(Deep breath.)* The irony is—unless we can come to some other arrangement, I'm gonna kill you! …That's the irony.

FELIX. What's wrong? *(Crosses back to tray, puts down glasses, etc.)*

OSCAR. There's something wrong with this system, that's what's wrong. I don't think that two single men living alone in a big eight-room apartment should have a cleaner house than my mother.

FELIX. *(Gets rest of dishes, glasses and coasters from table.)* What are you talking about? I'm just going to put the dishes in the sink. You want me to leave them here all night?

OSCAR. *(Takes his glass which FELIX has put on tray and crosses to bar for refill.)* I don't care if you take them to bed with you. You can play Mr. Clean all you want. But don't make *me* feel guilty.

FELIX. *(Takes tray into kitchen, leaving swinging door open.)* I'm not asking you to do it, Oscar. You don't have to clean up.

OSCAR. *(Moves up to door.)* *That's* why you make me feel guilty. You're always in my bathroom hanging up my towels… Whenever I smoke you follow me around with an ashtray… Last night I found you washing the kitchen floor shaking your head and moaning, "Footprints, footprints"! *(Paces right.)*

FELIX. *(Comes back to table with silent butler into which he dumps the ashtrays; then wipes them carefully.)* I didn't say they were yours.

OSCAR. *(Angrily; sits down right in wing chair.)* Well, *they were* mine, damn it. I have feet and they make prints. What do you want me to do, climb across the cabinets?

FELIX. No! I want you to walk on the floor.

OSCAR. I appreciate that! I really do.

FELIX. *(Crosses to telephone table and cleans ashtray there.)* I'm just trying to keep the place livable. I didn't realize I irritated you that much.

OSCAR. I just feel *I* should have the right to decide when my bathtub needs a going over with Dutch Cleanser... It's the democratic way!

FELIX. *(Puts down silent butler and rag on coffee table and sits down on couch, glumly.)* I was wondering how long it would take.

OSCAR. How long *what* would take?

FELIX. Before I got on your nerves.

OSCAR. I didn't say you get on my nerves.

FELIX. Well, it's the same thing. You said I irritated you.

OSCAR. *You* said you irritated me. *I* didn't say it.

FELIX. Then what *did* you say?

OSCAR. I don't know *what* I said. What's the difference what I said?

FELIX. It doesn't make any difference. I was just repeating what I thought you said.

OSCAR. Well, don't repeat what you *thought* I said. Repeat what I *said!* ...My God, that's irritating!

FELIX. You see! You *did* say it!

OSCAR. I don't believe this whole conversation. *(Gets up and paces above table.)*

FELIX. *(Pawing with a cup.)* Oscar, I'm—I'm sorry. I don't know what's wrong with me.

OSCAR. *(Paces down right.)* And don't pout. If you want to fight, we'll fight. But don't pout! Fighting *I* win. Pouting *you* win!

FELIX. You're right. Everything you say about me is absolutely right.

OSCAR. *(Really angry, turns to* **FELIX.***)* And don't give in so easily. I'm *not* always right. Sometimes *you're* right.

FELIX. You're right. I do that. I always figure I'm in the wrong.

OSCAR. Only this time you *are* wrong. And I'm right.

FELIX. Oh, leave me alone.

OSCAR. And don't sulk. That's the same as pouting.

FELIX. I know. I know. *(He squeezes cup with anger.)* Damn me, why can't I do one lousy thing right? *(He suddenly stands up and cocks his arm back angrily about to hurl the cup against the front door, then thinks better of it and puts it down and sits.)*

OSCAR. *(Watching this.)* Why didn't you throw it?

FELIX. I almost did. I get so insane with myself sometimes.

OSCAR. Then why don't you throw the cup?

FELIX. Because I'm trying to control myself.

OSCAR. Why?

FELIX. What do you mean, why?

OSCAR. Why do you have to control yourself? You're angry, you felt like throwing the cup, why don't you throw it?

FELIX. Because there's no point to it. I'd still be angry and I'd have a broken cup.

OSCAR. How do you *know* how you'd feel? Maybe you'd feel *wonderful.* Why do you have to control every single thought in your head? ...Why don't you let loose *once* in your life? Do something that you *feel* like doing—and not what you *think* you're supposed to do. Stop keeping books, Felix. Relax. Get drunk. Get angry... C'mon, *break the Goddamned cup!*

> *(**FELIX** suddenly stands up and hurls the cup against the door, smashing it to pieces. Then he grabs his shoulder in pain.)*

FELIX. Oww! ...I hurt my arm! *(Sinks down on couch, massaging his arm.)*

OSCAR. *(Throws up hands.)* You're hopeless! You're a hopeless mental case! *(Paces about the table.)*

FELIX. *(Grimacing with pain.)* I'm not supposed to throw with that arm. What a stupid thing to do.

OSCAR. Why don't you live in a closet? I'll leave your meals outside the door and slide in the papers. Is that safe enough?

FELIX. *(Rubbing arm.)* I used to have bursitis in this arm. I had to give up golf... Do you have a heating pad?

OSCAR. How can you hurt your arm throwing a cup? If it had coffee in it, that's one thing. But an *empty cup...* *(Sits in wing chair.)*

FELIX. All right, cut it out, Oscar. That's the way I am. I get hurt easily. I can't help it.

OSCAR. You're not going to cry, are you? I think all those tears dripping on the arm is what gave you bursitis.

FELIX. *(Holding arm.)* I once got it just from combing my hair.

OSCAR. *(Shaking his head.)* A world full of roommates and I pick myself the Tin Man. *(Sighs.)* Oh, well, I suppose I could have done worse.

FELIX. *(Puts rag and silent butler on bar. Takes chip box from bar and crosses to table.)* You're darn right, you could have. A *lot* worse.

OSCAR. *How?*

FELIX. What do you mean, how? How'd you like to live with Ten-thumbs Murray or Speed and his complaining? *(Gets down on his knees, picks up chips and puts them into box.)* Don't forget I cook and clean and take care of this house. I save us a lot of money, don't I?

OSCAR. Yeah, but then you keep me up all night counting it.

FELIX. *(Goes to table and sweeps chips and cards into box.)* Now wait a minute. We're not always going at each other. We have some fun too, don't we?

OSCAR. *(Crosses to couch.) Fun?* Felix, getting a clear picture on Channel Two isn't my idea of whoopee.

FELIX. What are you talking about?

OSCAR. All right, what do you and I do every night? *(Takes off sneakers, dropping them on floor.)*

FELIX. What do we do? You mean after dinner?

OSCAR. That's right. After we've had your halibut steak and the dishes are done and the sink has been Brillo'd and the pans have been S.O.S.'d and the leftovers have been Saran-wrapped—what do we do?

FELIX. *(Finishes clearing table and puts everything on top of bookcase.)* Well, we read…we talk…

OSCAR. *(Takes off pants and throws them on floor.)* No, no. *I* read and *you* talk! …I try to work and you talk… I take a bath and you talk… I go to sleep and you talk. We've got your life arranged pretty good but I'm still looking for a little entertainment.

FELIX. *(Pulling upstage kitchen chairs away from table.)* What are you saying? That I talk too much?

OSCAR. *(Sits on couch.)* No, no. I'm not complaining. You have a lot to say. What's worrying me is that I'm beginning to listen.

FELIX. *(Pulls table up into alcove.)* Oscar, I told you a hundred times, just tell me to shut up. I'm not sensitive. *(Pulls loveseat down into room, and centers table between windows in alcove.)*

OSCAR. I don't think you're getting my point. For a husky man, I think I've spent enough evenings discussing tomorrow's menu… The night was made for other things.

FELIX. Like what? *(Puts two dining chairs neatly at left and down of the table.)*

OSCAR. Like unless I get to touch something soft in the next two weeks, I'm in big trouble.

FELIX. You mean women? *(Puts two other dining chairs neatly at right and down of table.)*

OSCAR. If you want to give it a name, all right, women!

FELIX. *(Picks up two kitchen chairs and starts towards landing.)* That's funny. You know I haven't even *thought* about women in weeks.

OSCAR. I fail to see the humor.

FELIX. *(Stops.)* No, that's really strange. I mean when Frances and I were happy I don't think there was a girl on the street I didn't stare at for ten minutes. *(Crosses to up left kitchen door, pushes it open with back.)* I used to take the wrong subway home just following a pair of legs... But since we broke up, I don't even know what a woman looks like. *(Takes chairs into kitchen.)*

OSCAR. Well, either I could go downstairs and buy a couple of magazines...or I could make a phone call.

FELIX. *(From the kitchen, as he washes dishes.)* What are you saying?

OSCAR. *(Crosses to humidor on small table down right and takes cigar.)* I'm saying let's spend one night talking to someone with higher voices than us.

FELIX. You mean go out on a date?

OSCAR. Ya...

FELIX. Oh, well, I—I can't.

OSCAR. Why not?

FELIX. Well, it's all right for you. But I'm still married.

OSCAR. *(Paces towards kitchen door.)* You can *cheat* until the divorce comes through!

FELIX. It's not that. It's just that... I have no—no *feeling* for it. I can't explain it.

OSCAR. Try!

FELIX. *(Comes to doorway with brush and dish in hand.)* Listen, I intend to go out. I get lonely, too. But I'm just separated a few weeks. Give me a little time. *(Goes back to sink.)*

OSCAR. There isn't any time left. I saw TV Guide and there's nothing on this week! *(Paces into and through kitchen and out kitchen door on landing to down right.)* What am I asking you? All I want to do is have dinner with a couple of girls. You just have to eat and talk. It's not hard. You've eaten and talked before.

FELIX. *(In kitchen.)* Why do you need me? Can't you go out yourself?

OSCAR. Because I may want to come back here. And if we walk in and find you washing the windows, it puts a damper on things. *(Sits down right.)*

FELIX. *(Pokes head out of kitchen.)* I'll take a pill and go to sleep. *(Back into kitchen.)*

OSCAR. Why take a pill when you can take a girl?

FELIX. *(Comes out with aerosol bomb held high over his head, and circles the room spraying it.)* Because I'd feel guilty, that's why. Maybe it doesn't make any sense to you, but that's the way I feel. *(Puts bomb on bar and takes silent butler and rag into kitchen. Places them on sink and busily begins to wipe refrigerator.)*

OSCAR. Look, for all I care you can take her in the kitchen and make a blueberry pie. But I think it's a lot healthier than sitting up in your bed every night writing Frances' name all through the crossword puzzles... Just for one night, talk to another girl.

FELIX. *(Pushes loveseat carefully in position down right and sits; weakening.)* But—who would I call? The only single girl I know is my secretary and I don't think she likes me.

OSCAR. *(Jumps up and crouches next to FELIX.)* Leave that to me. There's two sisters who live in this building. English girls. One's a widow, the other's a divorcee. They're a barrel of laughs.

FELIX. How do you know?

OSCAR. I was trapped in the elevator with them last week. *(Runs to telephone table, puts directory on floor, and gets down on knees to look for number.)* I've been meaning to call them but I didn't know which one to take out. This'll be perfect.

FELIX. What do they look like?

OSCAR. Don't worry. Yours is very pretty.

FELIX. I'm not worried... Which one is mine?

OSCAR. The divorcée. *(Looking in book.)*

FELIX. *(Goes to OSCAR.)* Why do I get the divorcée?

OSCAR. I don't care. You want the widow? *(Circles number on page with crayon.)*

FELIX. *(Sitting on couch.)* No, I don't want the widow. I don't even want the divorcee. I'm just doing this for you.

OSCAR. Look, take whoever you want. When they come in the door, point to the sister of your choice. *(Tears page out of the book, runs to bookcase and hangs it up.)* I don't care. I just want to have some laughs.

FELIX. All right. All right.

OSCAR. *(Crosses to couch, sits next to FELIX.)* Don't say all right. I want you to promise me you're going to try to have a good time. Please, Felix. It's important. Say I promise.

FELIX. *(Nods.)* I promise.

OSCAR. Again!

FELIX. I promise!

OSCAR. And no writing in the book, a dollar thirty for the cab.

FELIX. No writing in the book.

OSCAR. No one is to be called Frances. It's Gwendolyn and Cecily.

FELIX. No Frances.

OSCAR. No crying, sighing, moaning or groaning.

FELIX. I'll smile from seven to twelve.

OSCAR. And this above all, no talk of the past. Only the present.

FELIX. And the future.

OSCAR. That's the new Felix I've been waiting for. *(Leaps up and prances right.)* Oh, is this going to be a night... Hey, where do you want to go?

FELIX. For what?

OSCAR. For dinner. Where'll we eat?

FELIX. You mean a restaurant? For the four of us? It'll cost a fortune.

OSCAR. We'll cut down on laundry. We don't wear socks on Thursdays.

FELIX. But that's throwing away money. We can't afford it, Oscar.

OSCAR. We have to eat.

FELIX. *(Moves to OSCAR.)* We'll have dinner here.

OSCAR. *Here?*

FELIX. I'll cook. We'll save thirty, forty dollars. *(He goes to couch, sits, and picks up phone.)*

OSCAR. What kind of a double date is that? You'll be in the kitchen all night.

FELIX. No, I won't. I'll put it up in the afternoon. Once I get my potatoes in, I'll have all the time in the world. *(He starts to dial.)*

OSCAR. *(Pacing back and forth.)* What happened to the new Felix? ...Who are you calling?

FELIX. Frances. I want to get her recipe for London broil. The girls'll be crazy about it.

>   *(He dials as OSCAR storms off towards his bedroom.)*
>
>   *(Curtain.)*

Scene Two

(TIME: A few days later. About 8 o'clock.)

(AT RISE: No one is onstage. The dining table looks like a page out of house and garden. It's set up for dinner for four, complete with linen tablecloth, candles and wine glasses. There is a floral centerpiece and flowers about the room, and crackers and dip on the coffee table. There are sounds of activity in the kitchen. The front door opens and **OSCAR** *enters with a bottle of wine in a brown paper bag, and his jacket over his arm. He looks about gleefully as he listens to the sounds from the kitchen. He puts the bag on the table and his jacket over the chair, down right.)*

OSCAR. *(Calls out. In a playful mood.)* I'm home, dear! *(He goes into his bedroom, taking off his shirt, and comes skipping out shaving with a cordless razor, and with a clean shirt and a tie over his arm. He is joyfully singing as he admires the table.)* Beautiful! Just beautiful! *(He sniffs, obviously catching the aroma from the kitchen.)* Oh, yeah. Something wonderful is going on in that kitchen... *(He rubs hands gleefully.)* No, sir. There's no doubt about it. I'm the luckiest man on earth.

(Puts razor into his pocket, and begins to put on shirt. **FELIX** *enters slowly from the kitchen. He's wearing a small dish towel as an apron. He has a ladle in one hand. He looks silently and glumly at* **OSCAR**, *crosses to the armchair and sits.)* I got the wine. *(Takes bottle out of the bag and puts it on the table.)*

Batard Montrachet. Six and a quarter. You don't mind, do you, pussycat? We'll walk to work this week.

*(***FELIX*** sits glumly and silently.)*

Hey, no kidding, Felix, you did a great job. One little suggestion? Let's come down a little with the lights...

(Switches off wall brackets.) and up very softly with the music.

> *(He crosses to stereo in bookcase and picks up albums.)*

OSCAR. What do you think goes better with London broil, Mancini or Sinatra?

> **(FELIX** *just stares ahead.)*

Felix?…What's the matter? *(Puts albums down.)* Something's wrong. I can tell by your conversation. *(Goes into bathroom, gets bottle of after shave lotion, comes out and puts it on.)* All right, Felix, what is it?

FELIX. *(Without looking at him.)* What is it? Let's start with what time do you think it is?

OSCAR. What time? I don't know. Seven-thirty?

FELIX. Seven-thirty? Try eight o'clock.

OSCAR. *(Puts lotion down on small table.)* All right, so it's eight o'clock. So? *(Begins to fix tie.)*

FELIX. So? …You said you'd be home at seven.

OSCAR. Is that what I said?

FELIX. *(Nods.)* That's what you said. "I will be home at seven" is what you said.

OSCAR. Okay, I said I'd be home at seven. And it's eight. So what's the problem?

FELIX. If you knew you were going to be late, why didn't you call me?

OSCAR. *(Pauses while making tie.)* I couldn't call you. I was busy.

FELIX. Too busy to pick up a phone? …Where were you?

OSCAR. I was in the office, working.

FELIX. *(Moves down left.)* Working? Ha!

OSCAR. Yes. Working!

FELIX. I called your office at seven o'clock. You were gone.

OSCAR. *(Tucking in shirt.)* It took me an hour to get home. I couldn't get a cab.

FELIX. Since when do they have cabs in Hannigan's bar?

OSCAR. Wait a minute. I want to get this down on a tape recorder…because no one'll believe me! …You mean now I have to call you if I'm coming home late for dinner?

FELIX. *(Crosses to* **OSCAR.***)* Not *any* dinner. Just the ones I've been slaving over since two o'clock this afternoon…to help save *you* money to pay your wife's alimony.

OSCAR. *(Controlling himself.)* Felix…this is no time to have a domestic quarrel. We have two girls coming down any minute.

FELIX. You mean you told them to be here at eight o'clock?

OSCAR. *(Takes jacket and crosses to couch. Sits and takes some dip from coffee table.)* I don't remember what I said. Seven-thirty, eight o'clock. What difference does it make?

FELIX. *(Follows* **OSCAR.***)* I'll tell you what difference. You told me they were coming at seven-thirty. You were going to be here at seven to help me with the hors d'oeuvres. At seven-thirty they arrive and we have cocktails. At eight o'clock we have dinner. It is now eight o'clock. *My-London-broil-is-finished!* If we don't eat now the whole damned thing'll be *dried out!*

OSCAR. Oh, God, help me.

FELIX. Never mind helping *you.* Tell him to save the meat. Because we got nine dollars and thirty-four cents worth drying up in there right now.

OSCAR. Can't you keep it warm?

FELIX. *(Paces right.)* What do you think I am, the Magic Chef? I'm lucky I got it to come out at eight o'clock. What am I going to do?

OSCAR. I don't know. Keep pouring gravy on it.

FELIX. What gravy?

OSCAR. Don't you have any gravy?

FELIX. *(Storms over to* **OSCAR.***)* Where the hell am I going to get gravy at eight o'clock?

OSCAR. *(Gets up and moves right.)* I thought it comes when you cook the meat.

FELIX. *(Follows him.)* When you *cook the meat?* You don't know the first thing you're talking about. You have to make gravy. It doesn't *come!*

OSCAR. You asked my advice, I'm giving it to you. *(Putting on jacket.)*

FELIX. Advice? *(He waves ladle in his face.)* You didn't know where the kitchen was 'til I came here and showed you.

OSCAR. You wanna talk to me, put down the spoon.

FELIX. *(Exploding in rage, again waving ladle in his face.)* Spoon? You dumb ignoramus. It's a ladle. You don't even know it's a ladle.

OSCAR. All right, Felix, get a hold of yourself.

FELIX. *(Pulls himself together, sits on loveseat.)* You think it's so easy? Go on. The kitchen's all yours. Go make a London broil for four people who come a half hour late.

OSCAR. *(To no one in particular.)* Listen to me. I'm arguing with him over gravy.

　　　(The bell rings.)

FELIX. *(Jumps up.)* Well, they're here. Our dinner guests. I'll get a saw and cut the meat. *(Starts for kitchen.)*

OSCAR. *(Stopping him.)* Stay where you are!

FELIX. I'm not taking the blame for this dinner.

OSCAR. Who's blaming you? Who even *cares* about the dinner?

FELIX. *(Moves to* OSCAR.*)* *I* care. I take *pride* in what I do. And you're going to explain to them exactly what happened.

OSCAR. All right, you can take a Polaroid picture of me coming in at eight o'clock! ...Now take off that stupid apron because I'm opening the door. *(Rips the towel off* FELIX *and goes to the door.)*

FELIX. *(Takes jacket from dining chair and puts it on.)* I just want to get one thing clear. This is the last time I ever cook for you. Because people like you don't even appreciate a decent meal. That's why they have T.V. dinners.

OSCAR. You through?

FELIX. I'm through!

OSCAR. Then smile.

> (**OSCAR** *smiles and opens the door. The girls poke their heads through the door. They are both in their young thirties and somewhat attractive. They are undoubtedly British.*)

Well, hello.

GWENDOLYN. *(To* **OSCAR.***)* Hallo!

CECILY. *(To* **OSCAR.***)* Hallo.

GWENDOLYN. I do hope we're not late.

OSCAR. No, no. You timed it perfectly. Come on in. *(He points to them as they enter.)* Er, Felix, I'd like you to meet two very good friends of mine, Gwendolyn and Cecily—

CECILY. *(Pointing out his mistake.)* Cecily and Gwendolyn.

OSCAR. Oh, yes. Cecily and Gwendolyn...er... *(Trying to remember their last name.)* Er... Don't tell me... Robin? ...No, no... Cardinal?

GWENDOLYN. Wrong both times. It's Pigeon!

OSCAR. Pigeon. Right. Cecily and Gwendolyn Pigeon.

GWENDOLYN. *(To* **FELIX.***)* You don't spell it like Walter Pidgeon. You spell it like "coo coo" pigeon.

OSCAR. We'll remember that if it comes up... Cecily and Gwendolyn, I'd like you to meet my roommate...and our chef for the evening... Felix Ungar.

CECILY. *(Holding hand out.)* Heh d'yew dew?

FELIX. *(Moving to her and shaking her hand.)* How do you do?

GWENDOLYN. *(Holding hand out.)* Heh d'yew dew?

FELIX. *(Stepping up on landing and shaking her hand.)* How do you do?

> (*This puts him nose to nose with* **OSCAR,** *and there is an awkward pause as they look at each other.*)

OSCAR. Well, we did that beautifully... Why don't we sit down and make ourselves comfortable?

>(FELIX *steps aside and ushers the girls down into the room. There is ad libbing and a bit of confusion and milling about as they all squeeze between the armchair and the couch, and the pigeons finally seat themselves on the couch.* OSCAR *sits in the armchair, and* FELIX *sneaks past him to the loveseat. Finally all have settled down.*)

CECILY. This is ever so nice, isn't it, Gwen?

GWENDOLYN. *(Looking around.)* Lovely. And much nicer than our flat. Do you have help?

OSCAR. Er, yes. I have a man who comes in every night.

CECILY. Aren't you the lucky one?

>(CECILY, GWENDOLYN *and* OSCAR *all laugh at her joke.* OSCAR *looks over at* FELIX *but there is no response.*)

OSCAR. *(Rubs hands together.)* Well, isn't this nice? ...I was telling Felix yesterday about how we happened to meet.

GWENDOLYN. Oh? ...Who's Felix?

OSCAR. *(A little embarrassed. Points to* FELIX.) He is!

GWENDOLYN. Oh, yes, of course. I'm so sorry.

>(FELIX *nods that it's all right.*)

CECILY. You know it happened to us again this morning.

OSCAR. What did?

GWENDOLYN. Stuck in the elevator again.

OSCAR. Really? Just the two of you?

CECILY. And poor old Mr. Kessler from the third floor. We were in there half an hour.

OSCAR. No kidding? What happened?

GWENDOLYN. Nothing much, I'm afraid.

>(CECILY *and* GWENDOLYN *both laugh at her latest joke, joined by* OSCAR. *He once again looks over at* FELIX, *but there is no response.*)

OSCAR. *(Rubs hands again.)* Well, this really is nice.

CECILY. And ever so much cooler than our place.

GWENDOLYN. It's like equatorial Africa on our side of the building.

CECILY. Last night it was so bad Gwen and I sat there in Nature's Own cooling ourselves in front of the open fridge. Can you imagine such a thing?

OSCAR. Er... I'm working on it.

GWENDOLYN. Actually, it's impossible to get a night's sleep. Cec and I really don't know what to do.

OSCAR. Why don't you sleep with an air conditioner?

GWENDOLYN. We haven't got one.

OSCAR. I know. But we have.

GWENDOLYN. Oh you! I told you about that one, didn't I, Cec?

FELIX. They say it may rain Friday.

(They all stare at **FELIX.***)*

GWENDOLYN. Oh?

CECILY. That should cool things off a bit.

OSCAR. I wouldn't be surprised.

FELIX. Although sometimes it gets hotter after it rains.

GWENDOLYN. Yes, it does, doesn't it?

(They continue to stare at **FELIX.***)*

FELIX. *(Jumps up and, picking up ladle, starts for the kitchen.)* Dinner is served!

OSCAR. *(Stopping him.)* No, it isn't!

FELIX. Yes, it is!

OSCAR. No, it isn't! I'm sure the girls would like a cocktail first. *(To girls.)* Wouldn't you, girls?

GWENDOLYN. Well, I wouldn't put up a struggle.

OSCAR. There you are. *(To* **CECILY.***)* What would you like?

CECILY. Oh, I really don't know. *(To* **OSCAR.***)* What have you got?

FELIX. London broil.

OSCAR. *(To* FELIX.*)* She means to drink. *(To* CECILY.*)* We have everything. And what we don't have, I mix in the medicine cabinet. What'll it be? *(Crouches next to her.)*

CECILY. Oh…a double vodka.

GWENDOLYN. Cecily…not before dinner.

CECILY. *(To the men.)* My sister… She watches over me like a mother hen. *(To* OSCAR.*)* Make it a *small* double vodka.

OSCAR. A small double vodka! …And for the beautiful mother hen?

GWENDOLYN. Oh… I'd like something cool. I think I would like to have a double Drambuie with some crushed ice…unless you don't have the crushed ice.

OSCAR. I was up all night with a sledge hammer… I shall return! *(Goes to bar and gets bottles of vodka and Drambuie.)*

FELIX. *(Going to him.)* Where are you going?

OSCAR. To get the refreshments.

FELIX. *(Starting to panic.)* Inside? What'll *I* do?

OSCAR. You can finish the weather report. *(He exits into kitchen.)*

FELIX. *(Calls after him.)* Don't forget to look at my meat! *(He turns and faces the girls. He crosses to chair and sits. He crosses his legs nonchalantly. But he is ill at ease and he crosses them again. He is becoming aware of the silence and he can no longer get away with just smiling.)* Er… Oscar tells me you're sisters.

CECILY. Yes. That's right. *(She looks at* GWENDOLYN.*)*

FELIX. From England.

GWENDOLYN. Yes. That's right. *(She looks at* CECILY.*)*

FELIX. I see. *(Silence. Then, his little joke.)* We're not brothers.

CECILY. Yes. We know.

FELIX. Although I am a brother. I have *a* brother who's a doctor. He lives in Buffalo. That's upstate in New York.

GWENDOLYN. *(Taking cigarette from her purse.)* Yes, we know.

FELIX. You know my brother?

GWENDOLYN. No. We know that Buffalo is upstate in New York.

FELIX. Oh!

>*(Gets up, takes cigarette lighter from side table and lights GWENDOLYN's cigarette.)*

CECILY. We've been there! ...Have you?

FELIX. No! ...Is it nice?

CECILY. Lovely.

>*(FELIX closes lighter on cigarette and turns to go back to chair, taking the cigarette, now caught in the lighter, with him. He notices cigarette and hastily gives it back to GWENDOLYN, stopping to light it once again. He puts lighter back on table and sits nervously. There is a pause.)*

FELIX. Isn't that interesting? ...How long have you been in the United States of America?

CECILY. Almost four years now.

FELIX. *(Nods.)* Uh-huh... Just visiting?

GWENDOLYN. *(Looks at CECILY.)* No! ...We live here.

FELIX. And you work here too, do you?

CECILY. Yes. We're secretaries for Slenderama.

GWENDOLYN. You know. The Health Club.

CECILY. People bring us their bodies and we do wonderful things with them.

GWENDOLYN. Actually, if you're interested, we can get you ten percent off.

CECILY. Off the price, not off your body.

FELIX. Yes, I see. *(He laughs, they all laugh. Suddenly shouts towards kitchen.)* Oscar, where's the drinks?

OSCAR. *(Offstage.)* Coming! Coming!

CECILY. What field of endeavor are you engaged in?

FELIX. I write the news for C.B.S.

CECILY. Oh! Fascinating!

GWENDOLYN. Where do you get your ideas from?

FELIX. *(He looks at her as though she's a Martian.)* From the news.

GWENDOLYN. Oh, yes, of course. Silly me...

CECILY. Maybe you can mention Gwen and I in one of your news reports.

FELIX. Well, if you do something spectacular, maybe I will.

CECILY. Oh, we've done spectacular things but I don't think we'd want it spread all over the Telly, do you, Gwen?

　　　　(They both laugh.)

FELIX. *(He laughs too, then cries out almost for help.)* Oscar!

OSCAR. *(Offstage.)* Yeah yeah!

FELIX. *(To girls.)* It's such a large apartment, sometimes you have to shout.

GWENDOLYN. Just you two baches live here?

FELIX. Baches? Oh, bachelors! We're not bachelors. We're divorced. That is, Oscar's divorced. I'm *getting* divorced.

CECILY. Oh. Small world. We've cut the dinghy loose too, as they say.

GWENDOLYN. Well, you couldn't have a *better* matched foursome, could you?

FELIX. *(Smiles weakly.)* No, I suppose not.

GWENDOLYN. Although technically, I'm a widow. I was divorcing my husband but he died before the final papers came through.

FELIX. Oh, I'm awfully sorry. *(Sighs.)* It's a terrible thing, isn't it? Divorce.

GWENDOLYN. It can be...if you haven't got the right solicitor.

CECILY. That's true. Sometimes they can drag it out for months. I was lucky. Snip, cut and I was free.

FELIX. I mean it's terrible what it can do to people. After all, what is divorce? It's taking two happy people and tearing their lives completely apart. It's inhuman, don't you think so?

CECILY. Yes, it can be an awful bother.

GWENDOLYN. But of course, that's all water under the bridge now, eh? ...er... I'm terribly sorry, but I think I've forgotten your name.

FELIX. Felix.

GWENDOLYN. Oh, yes. Felix.

CECILY. Like the Cat.

(FELIX *takes wallet from his jacket pocket.*)

GWENDOLYN. Well, the Pigeons will have to beware of the cat, won't they? *(She laughs.)*

CECILY. *(Nibbles on a nut from the dish.)* Mmm, cashews. Lovely.

FELIX. *(Takes snapshot out of wallet.)* This is the worst part of breaking up. *(He hands picture to* CECILY.*)*

CECILY. *(Looks at it.)* Childhood sweethearts, were you?

FELIX. No, no. That's my little boy and girl.

(CECILY *gives picture to* GWENDOLYN, *and takes pair of glasses from her purse and puts them on.*)

He's seven, she's five.

CECILY. *(Looks again.)* Oh! Sweet.

FELIX. They live with their mother.

GWENDOLYN. I imagine you must miss them terribly.

FELIX. *(Takes back picture and looks at it longingly.)* I can't stand being away from them. *(Shrugs.)* But—that's what happens with divorce.

CECILY. When do you get to see them?

FELIX. Every night. I stop there on my way home! ...Then I take them on the weekends and I get them on holidays and July and August.

CECILY. Oh! ...Well, when is it that you miss them?

FELIX. Whenever I'm not there. If they didn't have to go to school so early, I'd go over and make them breakfast. They love my French toast.

GWENDOLYN. You're certainly a devoted father.

FELIX. It's Frances who's the wonderful one.

CECILY. She's the little girl?

FELIX. No. She's the mother. My wife.

GWENDOLYN. The one you're divorcing?

FELIX. *(Nods.)* Mm! …She's done a terrific job bringing them up. They always look so nice. They're so polite. Speak beautifully. Never "Yeah." Always "Yes." …They're such good kids. And she did it all. She's the kind of woman who—Ah, what am I saying? You don't want to hear any of this. *(Puts picture back in wallet.)*

CECILY. Nonsense. You have a right to be proud. You have two beautiful children and a wonderful ex-wife.

FELIX. *(Containing his emotions.)* I know. I know. *(He hands* **CECILY** *another snapshot.)* That's her. Frances.

GWENDOLYN. *(Looking at picture.)* Oh, she's pretty. Isn't she pretty, Cecy?

CECILY. Oh, yes. Pretty. A pretty girl. Very pretty.

FELIX. *(Takes picture back.)* Thank you. *(Shows them another snapshot.)* Isn't this nice?

GWENDOLYN. *(Looks.)* There's no one in the picture.

FELIX. I know. It's a picture of our living room. We had a beautiful apartment.

GWENDOLYN. Oh, yes. Pretty. Very pretty.

CECILY. Those are lovely lamps.

FELIX. Thank you! *(Takes picture.)* We bought them in Mexico on our honeymoon… *(He looks at picture again.)* I used to love to come home at night. *(He's beginning to break.)* That was my whole life. My wife, my kids…and my apartment. *(He breaks down and sobs.)*

CECILY. Does she have the lamps now, too?

FELIX. *(Nods.)* I gave her everything… It'll never be like that again… Never! …I—I— *(He turns head away.)* I'm sorry.

> *(He takes out a handkerchief and dabs eyes.* **GWENDOLYN** *and* **CECILY** *look at each other with compassion.)*

Please forgive me. I didn't mean to get emotional. *(Trying to pull himself together. He picks up bowl from side table and offers it to* **GIRLS.***)* Would you like some potato chips?

>   *(***CECILY** *takes the bowl.)*

GWENDOLYN. You mustn't be ashamed. I think it's a rare quality in a man to be able to cry.

FELIX. *(Hand over eyes.)* Please. Let's not talk about it.

CECILY. I think it's sweet. Terribly terribly sweet. *(Takes potato chip.)*

FELIX. You're just making it worse.

GWENDOLYN. *(Teary-eyed.)* It's so refreshing to hear a man speak so highly of the woman he's divorcing! ...Oh, dear. *(She takes out her handkerchief.)* Now you've got me thinking about poor Sydney.

CECILY. Oh, Gwen. Please don't. *(Puts bowl down.)*

GWENDOLYN. It was a good marriage at first. Everyone said so. Didn't they, Cecily? Not like you and George.

CECILY. *(The past returns as she comforts* **GWENDOLYN.***)* That's right. George and I were never happy... Not for one single, solitary day. *(She remembers her unhappiness and grabs her handkerchief and dabs her eyes. All three are now sitting with handkerchiefs at their eyes.)*

FELIX. Isn't this ridiculous?

GWENDOLYN. I don't know what brought this on. I was feeling so good a few minutes ago.

CECILY. I haven't cried since I was fourteen.

FELIX. Just let it pour out. It'll make you feel much better. I always do.

GWENDOLYN. Oh dear oh dear oh dear.

>   *(All three sit sobbing into their handkerchiefs. Suddenly* **OSCAR** *bursts happily into the room with a tray full of drinks. He is all smiles.)*

OSCAR. *(Like a corny M.C.)* Is ev-rybuddy happy?

(Then he sees the maudlin scene. **FELIX** *and the girls quickly try to pull themselves together.)*

OSCAR. *(*What the hell happened?

FELIX. Nothing! Nothing! *(He quickly puts handkerchief away.)*

OSCAR. What do you mean, nothing? I'm gone three minutes and I walk into a funeral parlor. What did you say to them?

FELIX. I didn't say anything. Don't start in again, Oscar.

OSCAR. I can't leave you alone for five seconds. Well, if you really want to cry, go inside and look at your London broil.

FELIX. *(He rushes madly into the kitchen.)* Oh, my gosh! Why didn't you call me? I told you to call me.

OSCAR. *(Giving drink to* **CECILY.***)* I'm sorry, girls. I forgot to warn you about Felix. He's a walking soap opera.

GWENDOLYN. I think he's the dearest thing I ever met.

CECILY. *(Taking the glass.)* He's so sensitive. So fragile. I just want to bundle him up in my arms and take care of him.

OSCAR. *(Holds out* **GWENDOLYN**'s *drink. At this, he puts it back down on tray and takes a swallow from his own drink.)* Well, I think when he comes out of that kitchen you may have to.

> *(Sure enough,* **FELIX** *comes out of the kitchen onto the landing looking like a wounded puppy. With a protective kitchen glove, he holds a pan with the exposed London broil. Black is the color of his true love.)*

FELIX. *(Very calmly.)* I'm going down to the delicatessen. I'll be right back.

OSCAR. *(Going to him.)* Wait a minute. Maybe it's not so bad. Let's see it.

FELIX. *(Shows him.)* Here! Look! Nine dollars and thirty-four cents' worth of ashes! *(Pulls pan away. To girls.)* I'll get some corned beef sandwiches.

OSCAR. *(Trying to get a look at it.)* Give it to me! Maybe we can save some of it.

FELIX. *(Holding it away from* OSCAR.*)* There's nothing to save. It's all black meat. Nobody likes black meat! ...

OSCAR. Can't I even look at it?

FELIX. No, you can't look at it!

OSCAR. Why can't I look at it?

FELIX. If you looked at your watch before you wouldn't have to look at the black meat now! Leave it alone! *(Turns to go back into kitchen.)*

GWENDOLYN. *(Going to him.)* Felix...! Can *we* look at it?

CECILY. *(Turning to him, kneeling on couch.)* Please?

> (FELIX *stops in the doorway to kitchen. He hesitates for a moment. He likes them. Then he turns and wordlessly holds pan out to them.* GWENDOLYN *and* CECILY *inspect it wordlessly, and then turn away sobbing quietly. To* OSCAR.*)*

How about Chinese food?

OSCAR. A wonderful idea.

GWENDOLYN. I've got a better idea. Why don't we just make potluck in the kitchen?

OSCAR. A *much* better idea.

FELIX. I used up all the pots! *(Crosses to love seal and sits, still holding the pan.)*

CECILY. Well then, we can eat up in *our* place. We have tons of Horn and Hardart's.

OSCAR. *(Gleefully.)* That's the best idea I ever heard.

GWENDOLYN. Of course it's awfully hot up there. You'll have to take off your jackets.

OSCAR. *(Smiling.)* We can always open up a refrigerator.

CECILY. *(Gets purse from couch.)* Give us five minutes to get into our cooking things.

> (GWENDOLYN *gets purse from couch.*)

OSCAR. Can't you make it four? I'm suddenly starving to death.

(The GIRLS *are crossing to door.)*

GWENDOLYN. Don't forget the wine.

OSCAR. How could I forget the wine?

CECILY. And a corkscrew.

OSCAR. *And* a corkscrew.

GWENDOLYN. And Felix.

OSCAR. No, I won't forget Felix.

CECILY. Ta ta!

OSCAR. Ta ta!

GWENDOLYN. Ta ta!

(The girls exit.)

OSCAR. *(Throws a kiss at the closed door.)* You bet your sweet little crumpets, ta ta! *(He wheels around beaming and quickly gathers up the corkscrew from bar, the wine and the records.)* Felix, I love you. You've just overcooked us into one hell of a night. Come on, get the ice bucket. Ready or not, here we come. *(Runs to door.)*

FELIX. *(Sitting motionless.)* I'm not going!

OSCAR. What?

FELIX. I said I'm not going.

OSCAR. *(Crossing to* FELIX.*)* Are you out of your mind? …Do you know what's waiting for us up there? You've just been invited to spend the evening in a two-bedroom hot-house with the Coo Coo Pigeon Sisters! What do you mean you're not going?

FELIX. I don't know how to talk to them. I don't know what to say. I already told them about my brother in Buffalo. I've used up my conversation.

OSCAR. Felix, they're crazy about you. They told me! One of them wants to wrap you up and make a bundle out of you. You're doing better than *I* am! Get the ice bucket. *(Starts for door.)*

FELIX. Don't you understand? I cried! I cried in front of two women.

OSCAR. *(Stops.)* And they *loved* it! I'm thinking of getting hysterical. *(Goes to door.)* Will you get the ice bucket?

FELIX. But why did I cry? Because I felt guilty. Emotionally I'm still tied to Frances and the kids.

OSCAR. Well, untie the knot just for tonight, will you!

FELIX. I don't want to discuss it anymore. *(Starts for kitchen.)* I'm going to scrub the pots and wash my hair. *(Goes into kitchen and puts pan in sink.)*

OSCAR. *(Yelling.)* Your greasy pots and your greasy hair can wait. You're coming upstairs with me!

FELIX. *(In kitchen.)* I'm not! *I'm not!*

OSCAR. What am I going to do with two girls? Felix, don't do this to me. I'll never forgive you!

FELIX. I'm not going!

OSCAR. *(Screams.)* All right, damn you, I'll go without you! *(And he storms out the door and slams it. Then it opens and he comes in again.)* Are you coming?

FELIX. *(Comes out of kitchen looking at magazine.)* No.

OSCAR. You mean you're not going to make any effort to change… This is the person you're going to be…until the day you die.

FELIX. *(Sitting on couch.)* We are what we are.

OSCAR. *(Nods, then crosses to a window, pulls back drapes and opens window wide. Starts back to door.)* It's twelve floors, not eleven.

> *(He walks out as* FELIX *stares at the open windows.)*
>
> *(Curtain.)*

ACT III

Scene One

(TIME: The next evening about 7:30 p.m.)

(AT RISE: The room is once again set up for the poker game, with the dining table pulled down right, and the chairs set about it and the loveseat moved back beneath the windows in the alcove. **FELIX** *appears from the bedroom with a vacuum cleaner. He is doing a thorough job on the rug. As he vacuums around the table, the door opens and* **OSCAR** *comes in wearing a summer hat and carrying a newspaper. He glares at* **FELIX**, *still vacuuming, and shakes his head contemptuously, as he crosses behind* **FELIX**, *leaving his hat on the side table next to the armchair, and goes into his bedroom.* **FELIX** *is not aware of his presence. Then suddenly the power stops on the vacuum as* **OSCAR** *has obviously pulled the plug in the bedroom.* **FELIX** *tries switching the on button a few times, then turns to go back into bedroom. He stops and realizes what's happened as* **OSCAR** *comes back into the room.* **OSCAR** *takes a cigar out of his pocket and as he crosses in front of* **FELIX** *to the couch, he unwraps it and drops the wrappings carelessly on the floor. He then steps up on the couch and walks back and forth mashing down the pillows. Stepping down, he plants one foot on the armchair and then sits on the couch, taking a wooden match from the coffee table, striking it on the table, and*

*lighting his cigar. He flips the match onto the rug
and settles back to read his newspaper.* **FELIX** *has
watched this all in silence, and now carefully picks
up the cigar wrappings and the match and drops
them into* **OSCAR**'s *hat. He then dusts his hands
and takes the vacuum cleaner into the kitchen,
pulling the cord in after him.* **OSCAR** *takes the
wrappings from the hat and puts them in the butt-
filled ashtray on the coffee table. Then takes the
ashtray and dumps it on the floor. As he once more
settles down with his newspaper,* **FELIX** *comes out
of the kitchen carrying a tray with steaming dish
of spaghetti. As he crosses behind* **OSCAR** *to the
table, he smells it "deliciously" and passes it close
to* **OSCAR** *to make sure* **OSCAR** *smells the fantastic
dish he's missing. As* **FELIX** *sits and begins to eat,*
OSCAR *takes can of aerosol spray from the bar, and
circling the table sprays all about* **FELIX**, *puts can
down next to him and goes back to his newspaper.)*

FELIX. *(Pushing spaghetti away.)* All right, how much longer
is this gonna go on?

OSCAR. *(Reading his paper.)* Are you talking to me?

FELIX. That's right, I'm talking to you.

OSCAR. What do you want to know?

FELIX. I want to know if you're going to spend the rest
of your life not talking to me. Because if you are, I'm
going to buy a radio. *(No reply.)* Well? *(No reply.)* I see.
You're not going to talk to me. *(No reply.)* All right. Two
can play at this game. *(Pause.)* If you're not going to
talk to me, I'm not going to talk to you. *(No reply.)* I
can act childish too, you know. *(No reply.)* I can go on
without talking just as long as you can.

OSCAR. Then why the hell don't you shut up?

FELIX. Are you talking to me?

OSCAR. You had your chance to talk last night. I begged
you to come upstairs with me. From now on I never

want to hear a word from that shampooed head as long as you live. That's a warning, Felix.

FELIX. *(Stares at him.)* I stand warned... Over and out!

OSCAR. *(Gets up taking key out of his pocket and slams it on the table.)* There's a key to the back door. If you stick to the hallway and your room, you won't get hurt. *(Sits back down on couch.)*

FELIX. I don't think I gather the entire meaning of that remark.

OSCAR. Then I'll explain it to you. Stay out of my way.

FELIX. *(Picks up key and moves to couch.)* I think you're serious. I think you're really serious... Are you serious?

OSCAR. This is my apartment. Everything in my apartment is mine. The only thing here that's yours is you. Just stay in your room and speak softly.

FELIX. Yeah, you're serious... Well, let me remind you that I pay half the rent and I'll go into any room I want. *(He gets up angrily and starts towards hallway.)*

OSCAR. Where are you going?

FELIX. I'm going to walk around your bedroom.

OSCAR. *(Slams down newspaper.)* You stay out of there.

FELIX. *(Steaming.)* Don't tell me where to go. I pay a hundred and twenty dollars a month.

OSCAR. That was off-season. Starting tomorrow the rates are twelve dollars a day.

FELIX. All right. *(He takes some bills out of his pocket and slams them down on table.)* There you are. I'm paid up for today. Now I'm going to walk in your bedroom. *(He starts to storm off.)*

OSCAR. Stay out of there! Stay out of my room!

> *(He chases after him.* **FELIX** *dodges around the table as* **OSCAR** *blocks the hallway.)*

FELIX. *(Backing away, keeping table between them.)* Watch yourself! Just watch yourself, Oscar!

OSCAR. *(With a pointing finger.)* I'm warning you. You want to live here, I don't want to see you, I don't want to hear you and I don't want to smell your cooking. Now get this spaghetti off my poker table.

FELIX. Ha! Haha!

OSCAR. What the hell's so funny?

FELIX. It's not spaghetti. It's linguini!

>   (OSCAR *picks up the plate of linguini, crosses to
>   the doorway, and hurls it into the kitchen.*)

OSCAR. Now it's garbage! (*Paces above couch.*)

FELIX. (*Looks at* OSCAR *unbelievingly. What an insane thing
to do.*) You are crazy! ...I'm a neurotic nut but *you are
crazy!*

OSCAR. *I'm* crazy, heh? That's really funny coming from a
fruitcake like you.

FELIX. (*Goes to kitchen door and looks in at the mess. Turns back
to* OSCAR.) I'm not cleaning that up.

OSCAR. Is that a promise?

FELIX. Did you hear what I said? I'm not cleaning it up.
It's your mess. (*Looking into kitchen again.*) Look at it.
Hanging all over the walls.

OSCAR. (*Crosses up on landing and looks at kitchen door.*) I like
it. (*Closes door and paces right.*)

FELIX. (*Fumes.*) You'd just let it lie there, wouldn't you? Until
it turns hard and brown and...yich... It's disgusting...
I'm cleaning it up.

>   (*He goes into kitchen.* OSCAR *chases after him.
>   There is the sound of a struggle and falling pots.*)

OSCAR. (*Offstage.*) Leave it alone! ...You touch one strand of
that linguini—and I'm gonna punch you right in your
sinuses.

FELIX. (*Dashes out of kitchen with* OSCAR *in pursuit. Stops and
tries to calm* OSCAR *down.*) Oscar... I'd like you to take a
couple of phenobarbital.

OSCAR. (*Points.*) Go to your room! ...Did you hear what I
said? *Go to your room!*

FELIX. All right...let's everybody just settle down, heh? *(He puts his hand on* **OSCAR**'s *shoulder to calm him but* **OSCAR** *pulls away violently from his "touch.")*

OSCAR. If you want to live through this night, you'd better tie me up and lock your doors and windows.

FELIX. *(Sits at table with great pretense of calm.)* All right, Oscar, I'd like to know what's happened.

OSCAR. *(Moves towards him.)* What's *happened?*

FELIX. *(Hurriedly slides over to the next chair.)* That's right. Something must have caused you to go off the deep end like this. What is it? Something I said? Something I did? Heh? What?

OSCAR. *(Pacing.)* It's nothing you said. It's nothing you did. It's *you!*

FELIX. I see... Well, that's plain enough.

OSCAR. I could make it plainer but I don't want to hurt you.

FELIX. What is it, the cooking? The cleaning? The crying?

OSCAR. *(Moving towards him.)* I'll tell you exactly what it is. It's the cooking, cleaning and crying... It's the talking in your sleep, it's the moose calls that open your ears at two o'clock in the morning... I can't take it anymore, Felix. I'm crackin' up. Everything you do irritates me. And when you're not here, the things I know you're gonna do when you come in irritate me... You leave me little notes on my pillow. I told you a hundred times, I can't stand little notes on my pillow. "We're all out of Corn Flakes. F.U." ...It took me three hours to figure out that F.U. was Felix Ungar... It's not your fault, Felix. It's a rotten combination.

FELIX. I get the picture.

OSCAR. That's just the frame. The picture I haven't even painted yet... I got a typewritten list in my office of the "Ten Most Aggravating Things You Do That Drive Me Berserk." ...But last night was the topper. Oh, that was the topper. Oh, that was the ever loving lulu of all times.

FELIX. What are you talking about, the London broil?

OSCAR. No, not the London broil. I'm talking about those two lamb chops. *(He points upstairs.)* I had it all set up with that English Betty Boop and her sister and I wind up drinking tea all night and telling them *your* life story.

FELIX. *(Jumps up.)* Oho! So *that's* what's bothering you. That I loused up your evening!

OSCAR. After the mood you put them in, I'm surprised they didn't go out to Rockaway and swim back to England.

FELIX. Don't blame me. I warned you not to make the date in the first place.

(He makes his point by shaking his finger in OSCAR's *face.)*

OSCAR. Don't point that finger at me unless you intend to use it!

FELIX. *(Moves in nose to nose with* OSCAR.) All right, Oscar, get off my back. Get off! *Off!*

> *(Startled by his own actions,* FELIX *jumps back from* OSCAR, *warily circles him, crosses to the couch and sits.)*

OSCAR. What's this? A display of temper? I haven't seen you really angry since the day I dropped my cigar in your pancake batter. *(Starts towards the hallway.)*

FELIX. *(Threateningly.)* Oscar… You're asking to hear something I don't want to say. But if I say it, I think you'd better hear it.

OSCAR. *(Comes back to table, places both hands on it, leans towards* FELIX.) If you've got anything on your chest besides your chin, you'd better get it off.

FELIX. *(Strides to table, places both hands on it, leans towards* OSCAR. *They are nose to nose.)* All right, I warned you… You're a wonderful guy, Oscar. You've done everything for me. If it weren't for you, I don't know what would have happened to me. You took me in here, gave me a place to live and something to live for. I'll never forget you for that. You're tops with me, Oscar.

OSCAR. *(Motionless.)* If I've just been told off, I think I may have missed it.

FELIX. It's coming now! ...You're also one of the biggest slobs in the world.

OSCAR. I see.

FELIX. And completely unreliable.

OSCAR. Finished?

FELIX. Undependable.

OSCAR. Is that it?

FELIX. And irresponsible.

OSCAR. Keep going. I think you're hot.

FELIX. That's it. I'm finished. *Now* you've been told off. How do you like that? *(Crosses to couch.)*

OSCAR. *(Straightening up.)* Good. Because now I'm going to tell *you* off... For six months I lived alone in this apartment. All alone in eight rooms... I was dejected, despondent and disgusted... Then *you* moved in. My dearest and closest friend... And after three weeks of close, personal contact—I am about to have a nervous breakdown! ...Do me a favor. Move into the kitchen. Live with your pots, your pans, your ladle and your meat thermometer... When you want to come out, ring a bell and I'll run into the bedroom. *(Almost breaking down.)* I'm asking you nicely, Felix... As a friend... Stay out of my way! *(And he goes into the bedroom.)*

FELIX. *(Hurt by this; then remembering something. Calls after him.)* Walk on the paper, will you? The floors are wet.

> *(OSCAR comes out of the door. He is glaring maniacally, as he slowly strides back down the hallway FELIX quickly puts the couch between him and OSCAR.)*

Awright, keep away. Keep away from me.

OSCAR. *(Chasing him around the couch.)* Come on. Let me get in one shot. You pick it. Head, stomach, or kidneys.

FELIX. *(Dodging about the room.)* You're gonna find yourself in one sweet law suit, Oscar.

OSCAR. It's no use running, Felix. There's only eight rooms and I know the short cuts.

>   (*They are now poised at opposite ends of the couch.*
>   **FELIX** *picks up a lamp for protection.*)

FELIX. Is this how you settle your problems, Oscar? Like an animal?

OSCAR. All right. You wanna see how I settle my problems. I'll show you. (*Storms off into* **FELIX**'s *bedroom. There is the sound of falling objects and he returns with a suitcase.*) I'll show you how I settle them. (*Throws suitcase on table.*) There! That's how I settle them!

FELIX. (*Bewildered, looks at suitcase.*) Where are you going?

OSCAR. (*Exploding.*) Not me, you idiot! You. You're the one who's going. I want you out of here. Now! Tonight! (*Opens suitcase.*)

FELIX. What are you talking about?

OSCAR. It's all over, Felix. The whole marriage. We're getting an annulment! Don't you understand? I don't want to live with you any more. I want you to pack your things, tie it up with your Saran Wrap and get out of here.

FELIX. You mean actually move out…?

OSCAR. Actually, physically and immediately. I don't care where you go. Move into the Museum of Natural History. (*Goes into kitchen. There is the crash of falling pots and pans.*) I'm sure you'll be very comfortable there. You can dust around the Egyptian mummies to your heart's content. But I'm a human living person. (*Comes out with stack of cooking utensils which he throws into the open suitcase.*) All I want is my freedom. Is that too much to ask for? (*Closes it.*) There… You're all packed.

FELIX. You know, I've got a good mind to really leave.

OSCAR. (*Looking to the heavens.*) Why doesn't he ever listen to what I say? Why doesn't he hear me? I know I'm talking… I recognize my voice.

FELIX. *(Indignantly.)* Because if you really want me to go, I'll go.

OSCAR. Then go. I want you to go, so go. When are you going?

FELIX. When am I going, huh? Boy, you're in a bigger hurry than Frances was...

OSCAR. Take as much time as she gave you. I want you to follow your usual routine.

FELIX. In other words you're throwing me out.

OSCAR. Not in other words. Those are the perfect ones. *(Picks up suitcase and holds it out to* **FELIX.***)* I am throwing you out.

FELIX. All right... I just wanted to get the record straight. Let it be on *your* conscience. *(Goes into his bedroom.)*

OSCAR. What...? What...? *(Follows him to bedroom doorway.)* Let what be on my conscience?

FELIX. *(Comes out putting on jacket, goes by* **OSCAR.***)* That you're throwing me out. *(Stops and turns back to him.)* I'm perfectly willing to stay and clear the air of our differences... But you refuse, right?

OSCAR. *(Still holding suitcase.)* Right... I'm sick and tired of you clearing the air. That's why I want you to leave!

FELIX. Okay... As long as I heard you say the words, "Get out of the house." ...Fine... But remember, what happens to me is your responsibility. Let it be on *your* head. *(Crosses to the door.)*

OSCAR. *(Follows him to door; screams.)* Wait a minute, damn it! Why can't you be thrown out like a decent human being? Why do you have to say things like, "Let it be on your head"? I don't want it on my head. I just want you out of the house.

FELIX. What's the matter, Oscar? Can't cope with a little guilt feelings—?

OSCAR. *(Pounding railing in frustration.)* Damn you. I've been looking forward to throwing you out all day long and now you even take the pleasure out of that.

FELIX. Forgive me for spoiling your fun. I'm leaving now… according to your wishes and desires. *(Starts to open the door.)*

OSCAR *(Pushes by* **FELIX** *and slams the door shut. Stands between* **FELIX** *and the door.)* You're not leaving here until you take it back.

FELIX. Take what back?

OSCAR. "Let it be on your head." …What the hell is that, the Curse of the Cat People?

FELIX. Get out of my way, please.

OSCAR. Is this how you left that night with Frances? No wonder she wanted to have the room repainted right away. *(Points to* **FELIX**'s *bedroom.)* I'm gonna have yours dipped in bronze.

FELIX. *(Sits on back of couch with his back to* **OSCAR**.*)* How can I leave if you're blocking the door?

OSCAR. *(Very calmly.)* Felix, we've been friends a long time. For the sake of that friendship, please say, "Oscar, we can't stand each other, let's break up."

FELIX. I'll let you know what to do about my clothes… Either I'll call…or someone else will. *(Controlling great emotion.)* I'd like to leave now.

> **(OSCAR,** *resigned, moves out of the way.* **FELIX** *opens the door.)*

OSCAR. Where will you go?

FELIX. *(Turns in doorway and looks at him.)* Where? … *(He smiles.)* Oh, come on, Oscar. You're not really interested, are you? *(He exits.)*

> **(OSCAR** *looks as though he's about to burst with frustration. He calls after* **FELIX**.*)*

OSCAR. All right, Felix, you win. *(Goes out into hall.)* We'll try to iron it out. Anything you want. Come back, Felix… Felix…? *Felix?* Don't leave me like this. —You louse!

> *(But* **FELIX** *is gone.* **OSCAR** *comes back into the room closing the door. He is limp. He searches for something to ease his enormous frustration. He*

*throws a pillow at the door, and then paces about
like a caged lion.)*

All right, Oscar, get ahold of yourself! …He's gone!
Keep saying that over and over… He's gone. He's really
gone! *(He holds his head in pain.)* He did it. He put a
curse on me. It's on my head. I don't know what it is,
but something's on my head. *(The doorbell rings and he
looks up hopefully.)* Please let it be him. Let it be Felix.
Please give me one more chance to kill him.

*(Putting the suitcase on the sofa, he rushes to
the door and opens it. MURRAY comes in with
VINNIE.)*

MURRAY. *(Putting jacket on chair at table.)* Hey, what's the
matter with Felix? He walked right by me with that
"human sacrifice" look on his face again. *(Takes off
shoes.)*

VINNIE. *(Laying jacket on loveseat.)* What's with him? I asked
him where he's going and he said, "Only Oscar knows.
Only Oscar knows." Where's he going, Oscar?

OSCAR. *(Sitting at table.)* How the hell should I know? All
right, let's get the game started, heh? Come on, get
your chips.

MURRAY. I have to get something to eat. I'm starving.
Mmm, I think I smell spaghetti. *(Goes into kitchen.)*

VINNIE. Isn't he playing tonight? *(Takes two chairs from
dining alcove and puts them downstage of table.)*

OSCAR. I don't want to discuss it. I don't even want to hear
his name.

VINNIE. Who? Felix?

OSCAR. I told you not to mention his name.

VINNIE. I didn't know what name you meant. *(Clears table
and places what's left from FELIX's dinner on bookcase.)*

MURRAY. *(Comes out of the kitchen.)* Hey, did you know there's
spaghetti all over the kitchen?

OSCAR. Yes, I know and it's not spaghetti, it's linguini.

MURRAY. Oh. I thought it was spaghetti. *(He goes back into the kitchen.)*

VINNIE. *(Taking poker stuff from bookcase and putting it on table.)* Why shouldn't I mention his name?

OSCAR. Who?

VINNIE. Felix. What's happened? Has something happened?

(SPEED and ROY come in the open door.)

SPEED. Yeah, what's the matter with Felix?

(SPEED puts his jacket over a chair at the table. ROY sits in armchair. MURRAY comes out of the kitchen with a six-pack of beer and bags of pretzels and chips. They all stare at OSCAR waiting for an answer. There is a long pause and then he stands up.)

OSCAR. We broke up! I kicked him out. It was my decision. I threw him out of the house. All right? …I admit it. Let it be on my head.

VINNIE. Let what be on your head?

OSCAR. *How should I know? Felix put it there! Ask him! (Paces right.)*

MURRAY. He'll go to pieces. I know Felix. He's gonna try something crazy.

OSCAR. *(Turns to boys.)* Why do you think I did it?

(MURRAY makes a gesture of disbelief and moves to couch, putting down beer and bags. OSCAR moves to him.)

You think I'm just selfish? That I wanted to be cruel? I did it for you… I did it for all of us.

ROY. What are you talking about?

OSCAR. *(Crosses to ROY.)* All right, we've all been through the napkins and the ashtrays and the bacon, lettuce and tomato sandwiches… But that was just the beginning. Just the beginning. Do you know what he was planning for next Friday night's poker game? As a change of pace. Do you have any idea?

VINNIE. What?

OSCAR. A Luau! An Hawaiian Luau! Spareribs, roast pork and fried rice... They don't play poker like that in Honolulu.

MURRAY. One thing has nothing to do with the other. We all know he's impossible but he's still our friend and he's still out on the street, and I'm still worried about him.

OSCAR. *(Going to* **MURRAY.***)* And I'm not, heh? I'm not concerned? I'm not worried? Who do you think sent him out there in the first place?

MURRAY. Frances!

OSCAR. What?

MURRAY. Frances sent him out in the first place. *You* sent him out in the second place. And whoever he lives with next will send him out in the third place... Don't you understand? It's Felix. He does it to himself.

OSCAR. Why?

MURRAY. I don't know why. *He* doesn't know why. There are people like that. There's a whole tribe in Africa who hit themselves on the head all day long. *(He sums it all up with an eloquent gesture of resignation.)*

OSCAR. *(A slow realization of a whole new reason to be angry.)* I'm not going to worry about him. Why should I? He's not worrying about me. He's somewhere out on the streets sulking and crying and having a wonderful time... If he had a spark of human decency he would leave us all alone and go back to Blanche. *(Sits down at table.)*

VINNIE. Why should he?

OSCAR. *(Picks up deck of cards.)* Because it's his wife.

VINNIE. No, Blanche is your wife. His wife is Frances.

OSCAR. *(Stares at him.)* What are you, some kind of wise guy?

VINNIE. What did I say?

OSCAR. *(Throws cards in air.)* All right, the poker game is over. I don't want to play any more. *(Paces right.)*

SPEED. Who's playing? We didn't even start.

OSCAR. *(Turns on him.)* Is that all you can do is complain? Have you given one single thought to where Felix might be?

SPEED. I thought you said you're not worried about him?

OSCAR. *(Screams.)* I'm not worried, dammit! I'm not worried. *(The doorbell rings. A gleeful look passes over* **OSCAR***'s face.)* It's him. I bet it's him! *(The boys start to go for the door.* **OSCAR** *stops them.)* Don't let him in, he's not welcome in this house.

MURRAY. *(Moves towards door.)* Oscar, don't be childish. We've got to let him in.

OSCAR. *(Stopping him and leading him to the table.)* I won't give him the satisfaction of knowing we've been worrying about him. Sit down. Play cards. Like nothing happened.

MURRAY. But, Oscar—

OSCAR. Sit down. Everybody... Come on... Sit down and play poker.

> *(They sit and* **SPEED** *begins to deal out cards.)*

VINNIE. *(Crossing to door.)* Oscar...

OSCAR. All right, Vinnie, open the door.

> **(VINNIE** *opens door. It is* **GWENDOLYN** *standing there.)*

VINNIE. *(Surprised.)* Oh, hello. *(To* **OSCAR***.)* It's not him, Oscar.

GWENDOLYN. How do you do? *(She walks into the room.)*

OSCAR. *(Crosses to her.)* Oh, hello, Cecily. Boys, I'd like you to meet Cecily Pigeon.

GWENDOLYN. Gwendolyn Pigeon. Please don't get up. *(To* **OSCAR***.)* May I see you for a moment, Mr. Madison? Oscar. Certainly, Gwen. What's the matter? Gwendolyn. I think you know... I've come for Felix's things.

> **(OSCAR** *looks at her in shock and disbelief. He looks at the Boys, then back at* **GWENDOLYN***.)*

OSCAR. Felix... My Felix?

GWENDOLYN. Yes. Felix Ungar. That sweet, tortured man who's in my flat at this moment pouring his heart out to my sister.

OSCAR. *(Turns to boys.)* You hear? I'm worried to death and he's up there getting tea and sympathy.

> *(CECILY rushes in dragging a reluctant FELIX with her.)*

CECILY. Gwen, Felix doesn't want to stay. Please tell him to stay.

FELIX. Really, girls, this is very embarrassing. I can go to a hotel... *(To boys.)* Hello, fellas.

GWENDOLYN. *(Overriding his objections.)* Nonsense. I told you, we've plenty of room, and it's a very comfortable sofa. Isn't it, Cecy?

CECILY. *(Joining in.)* Enormous. And we've rented an air-conditioner.

GWENDOLYN. And we just don't like the idea of you wandering the streets looking for a place to live.

FELIX. But I'd be in the way. Wouldn't I be in the way?

GWENDOLYN. How could you possibly be in anyone's way?

OSCAR. You want to see a typewritten list?

GWENDOLYN. *(Turning on him.)* Haven't you said enough already, Mr. Madison? *(To FELIX.)* I won't take no for an answer. Just for a few days, Felix.

CECILY. Until you get settled.

GWENDOLYN. Please. Please say "Yes," Felix.

CECILY. Oh, please...we'd be so happy.

FELIX. *(Considers.)* Well...maybe just for a few days.

GWENDOLYN. *(Jumping with joy.)* Oh, wonderful.

CECILY. *(Ecstatic.)* Marvelous!

GWENDOLYN. *(Crosses to door.)* You get your things and come right up.

CECILY. And come hungry. We're making dinner.

GWENDOLYN. *(To boys.)* Good night, gentlemen, sorry to interrupt your bridge game.

CECILY. *(To* **FELIX.***)* If you'd like, you can invite your friends to play in our flat.

GWENDOLYN. *(To* **FELIX.***)* Don't be late. Cocktails in fifteen minutes.

FELIX. I won't.

GWENDOLYN. Ta ta.

CECILY. Ta ta.

FELIX. Ta ta.

> *(The girls leave.* **FELIX** *turns and looks at the fellows and smiles as he crosses the room into the bedroom. The five men stare dumbfounded at the door without moving. Finally* **MURRAY** *crosses to the door.)*

SPEED. *(To the others.)* I told you. It's always the quiet guys.

MURRAY. Gee, what nice girls. *(Closes door.)*

> *(***FELIX** *comes out of the bedroom carrying two suits in a plastic cleaner's bag.)*

ROY. Hey, Felix, are you really gonna move in with them?

FELIX. *(Turns back to them.)* Just for a few days. Until I find my own place… Well, so long, fellows. You can drop your crumbs on the rug again. *(Starts towards door.)*

OSCAR. Hey, Felix. Aren't you going to thank me?

FELIX. *(Stopping on landing.)* For what?

OSCAR. For the two greatest things I ever did for you. Taking you in and throwing you out.

FELIX. *(Lays suits over railing and goes to* **OSCAR.***)* You're right, Oscar. Thanks a lot. Getting kicked out twice is enough for any man… In gratitude, I remove the curse.

OSCAR. *(Smiles.)* Oh, bless you and thank you. Wicked Witch of the North.

> *(They shake hands. The phone rings.)*

FELIX. Ah, that must be the girls.

MURRAY. *(Picking up phone.)* Hello…

FELIX. They hate it so when I'm late for cocktails. *(Turning to boys.)* Well, so long.

MURRAY. It's your wife.

FELIX. *(Turning to* **MURRAY.***)* Oh? Well, do me a favor, Murray. Tell her I can't speak to her now. But tell her I'll be calling her in a few days because she and I have a lot to talk about. And tell her if I sound different to her, it's because I'm not the same man she kicked out three weeks ago. Tell her, Murray, tell her.

MURRAY. I will when I see her. This is Oscar's wife.

FELIX. Oh!

MURRAY. *(Into phone.)* Just a minute, Blanche.

> *(***OSCAR** *crosses to phone, sits on arm of the couch.)*

FELIX. Well, so long, fellows. *(Shakes hands with the boys, takes suits and moves to door.)*

OSCAR. *(Into phone.)* Hello? …Yeah, Blanche. I got a pretty good idea why you're calling. You got my checks, right? …Good.

> *(***FELIX** *stops at the door, caught by* **OSCAR**'*s conversation. He slowly comes back into the room to listen, putting suits on railing, and sitting down on the arm of the armchair.)*

So now I'm all paid up… No, no, I didn't win at the track. I've just been able to save a little money… I've been eating home a lot. *(Takes a pillow from couch and throws it at* **FELIX.***)* Listen, Blanche, you don't have to thank me. I'm just doing what's right… Well, that's nice of you, too… The apartment? No, I think you'd be shocked… It's in surprisingly good shape…

> *(***FELIX** *throws pillow back at* **OSCAR.***)*

Say, Blanche, did Brucey get the goldfish I sent him? …Yeah, well, I'll speak to you again soon, huh? … Whenever you want. I don't go out much any more…

FELIX. *(Gets up, takes suits from railing and goes to door.)* Well, good night, Mr. Madison. If you need me again, I get a dollar-fifty an hour.

OSCAR. *(Makes gesture to stop* FELIX *as he talks on phone.)* Well, kiss the kids for me. Good night, Blanche. *(Hangs up and turns to* FELIX.*)* Felix? ...

FELIX. *(At opened door.)* Yeah?

OSCAR. How about next Friday night? You're not going to break up the game, are you?

FELIX. Me? Never! Marriages may come and go, but the game must go on. So long, Frances. *(He exits, closing door.)*

OSCAR. *(Yelling after him.)* So long, Blanche. *(The boys all look at* OSCAR *a moment.)* All right, are we just gonna sit around or are we gonna play poker?

ROY. We're gonna play poker.

> *(There is a general hubbub as they pass out the beer, deal the cards, etc.)*

OSCAR. *(Standing up.)* Then let's play poker. *(Sharply the boys.)* And watch your cigarettes, will you? This is my house, not a pig sty.

> *(Takes the ashtray from the side table next to armchair, bends down and begins to pick up the butts. The* BOYS *settle down to play poker.)*

> *(Curtain.)*

WORKING PROP LIST

ACT ONE

ON STAGE:

Furniture:

Print side chair (downstage right)

Small round side table (downstage right)

Round wooden dining table (downstage right center)

2 red, open-backed, wooden kitchen chairs (downstage of table)

4 matched straight wooden dining chairs (right, left and upstage of table)

Small, console table, right wall (between bathroom and bedroom)

Brick side chair (center stage left of poker table)

Loveseat (upstage center, angled in dining alcove)

Pedestal table (upstage center between two windows)

Console table (used as bar) (upstage left center, against wall)

Plaid upholstered armchair (left stage center)

Upholstered couch (downstage left center, left of armchair)

Coffee table (downstage of couch)

Large round end table (left of couch)

Wooden chest (in niche on landing)

Standing lamp (upstage right at poker table)

Standing ash tray (with butts) (between bookcase and loveseat)

Extra piece of rug, center

PROPS AND DRESSING:

By Upholstered Chair (downstage right):

Striped pillow on floor, on scattered newspapers, leaning against chair

Beige banlon shirt over back of chair

On Round Side Table (downstage right):
 1 man's rain hat, leaning on beer can (empty)
 1 green and white cigarette box
 1 brass ash tray (with butts)

On Console Table (right wall):
 Oval tray (leaning against wall)
 Three books
 Newspaper (on top of books)
 Open decanter
 Old, electric fan (practical) (elec.)

Hanging in Alcove, from Bookcase:
 Toy airplane

On stage right Bedroom Door Frame:
 Wooden hanger with ties (downstage corner of frame)

On Hallway Bookcase:
 3 wire hangers, with clothes (hanging on downstage corner)
 Brass lamp
 Doll on 2 books
 2 thin books

On Bookshelves, stage right. (floor to ceiling):
 Stereo set, with speakers
 Collection of record albums (lower shelf)
 Wooden hanger, with pants and suspenders (hanging from 7th shelf)
 Books (Special book, 5th shelf from bottom)
 3 record album covers, on floor, leaning against speaker

On Bookcase (under window, right):
 Pile of record albums
 Typewriter (on record albums)
 2 empty cigarette cartons (on typewriter)
 Dead fern in brass planter
 Ceramic ash tray (with butts)
 Newspaper
 Plate of bread pieces (on newspaper)
 2 empty liquor bottles
 1 empty Pepsi bottle

1 empty Coca-Cola bottle

Kitty box (cigar box), with bills (on empty cigar box)

Towel (behind cigar box)

1 empty beer can

1 glass, with very little water in it, downstage left corner

On Dining Table (poker table):

5 groups of poker chips (in stacks):

(Large stacks right)

(Small stacks, upstage right, upstage left, left, and downstage right)

1 apple (upstage right)

1 deck of blue cards (upstage right)

1 deck of red cards (upstage left)

1 bowl of fruit, with stale fruit, bananas, apples, etc. (upstage center)

2 ash trays, with butts (right and left)

1 empty Coke bottle (upstage right)

2 empty beer cans (right and upstage left)

Cigarettes and matches (right)

Cigar and matches (upstage left)

Cigar and matches (downstage right)

1 overfilled bag of potato chips (left)

1 open full beer can (left)

On Standing Lamp:

Towel

On Brick Side Chair, center:

One sock and garter

Pair of black shoes on floor, right and left of right leg

Beer can in shoe left of right leg

Newspaper under chair

On Plaid Armchair (left center stage:

Matching pillow

Laundry bag, with clothes hanging out of it

Brown pants over right arm and back of chair

Standing ash tray, left of bookcase, right of loveseat (with butts)

On Loveseat:

    1 white shirt, over downstage arm
    1 brown embroidered pillow
    1 round velvet pillow
    1 gold damask pillow
    Newspapers on floor downstage of loveseat

On Air Conditioner:

    Blue shirt

On Pedestal Table (between windows):

    2 empty beer cans
    1 empty Pepsi bottle
    1 empty Coca-Cola bottle
    Gold cigarette box
    Picture of baseball batter in frame

On Ledge of Window, left:

    1 empty beer can
    1 empty milk carton

On Console Table (upstage left center) (bar):

    4 bottles of liquor (various levels of contents)
    4 glasses, filled to various levels
    4 empty (clean) glasses
    2 empty Coca-Cola bottles
    Ice bucket, top off
    Red and black diamond tie draped over lamp shade, on lamp
    Ash tray, with butts
    5 empty beer cans

On Floor, downstage of Bar:

    Wastebasket
    Large paper bag, with trash, on top of wastebasket
    Old shirt board, between wastebasket and wall

On Couch:

    2 pillows (one in each corner)
    1 pair black pants, over back of couch

On Floor, right of Couch:

    Magazine rack, with magazines and papers disarrayed
    Scattered newspapers

On Coffee Table:

  2 sports magazines (at right side of table)

  1 blue ash tray, with butts, and 1 fresh cigar (not in wrapper) (on
    magazines)

  2 books matches (on magazines)

  1 empty TV dinner tray, with banana (on magazines)

  Flat trash (shirt boards, paper, etc.) (at left side of table)

Under Coffee Table:

  3 magazines (right)

  1 empty TV dinner tray (on magazines)

  1 cup in 1 bowl in 1 plate (left)

On *Round Table, left of Couch:*

  Lamp (burnt hole lamp shade, facing downstage) (elec.)

  Phone

  Empty coffee containers

  Green ash tray, with butts

  Pile of mail

On Floor, Under Round Table, left:

  1 pair brown shoes

  Telephone book

  Wastebasket, full

  Paisley pillow, on phone book, leaning against wastebasket

Portable TV on Stand, Against Wall, downstage left

On Chest (on landing):

  Laundry packages (some loose shirts on top)

  Vase

  Hat on vase

  Blue box

  Pile of mail

On Floor, Under TV, and on Landing, left:

  Scattered newspapers

On Railing:

  Raincoat

On upstage center Wall Jog:

  2 pots of dead ivy (1 on downstage side, 1 on upstage side)

Windows:

Drapes open

Windows open

Venetian blinds, half up

Venetian blind over bookcase, fanned

OFF STAGE:

Left, Outside Front Door:

Two trash cans. Top off of one

Off Stage in Kitchen, upstage left:

Sink, with practical water

Refrigerator

Small table, right

Large tray, on refrigerator, containing:

Opened bag of pretzels, half filled

Opened bag of Fritos, half filled

Plate with stack (8) of green and brown sandwiches

2 empty plates

Small unopened bottle of Coca-Cola

3 unopened cans of beer

Can and bottle opener

Unopened small can of peanuts, with key

On refrigerator:

Unopened bottle of Coca-Cola (root beer)

Empty, clean glass

Bottle opener

Dishes, utensils, etc, in sink and on drainboard

OFF STAGE RIGHT:

Upstage right in bedroom:

Chest, with lamp

Sweat shirt on chest

Tie and checked shirt hanging out top drawer of chest

Blue shirt hanging out 2nd drawer of chest

Right in bedroom:

Chest, with lamp

Pillow and pillow case (not folded) on chest

Pair of pajamas on hook

Downstage Right in bathroom:

    Sink

    Medicine cabinet on upstage wall

    Towel, disarrayed, over towel rack, upstage wall

    Wet face cloth on sink

    Bottle of after-shave lotion on sink

CHECK LIST:

    Chairs at poker table on marks

    All windows and drapes open

Doors open:

    Bedroom, upstage right

    Bedroom, right

    Bedroom to bathroom, right

    Bathroom, downstage right

Doors closed:

    Swinging door to kitchen

    Kitchen door on landing

    Front door

    Door on landing, outside front door

ACT TWO

Scene One

STRIKE:

> Fan (elec.)
> All debris and dressing
> Dead fern
> 2 dead pots ivy
> Standing ash tray
> Ceramic ash tray from bookcase
> Wastebasket from under phone table
> Empty butts from blue ash tray (coffee table)
> Extra piece of rug

RE-SET:

> 2 kitchen chairs to upstage right and upstage left of poker table
> 2 dining chairs to downstage right and downstage left of poker table
> Brick side chair (from center) to left of downstage right side table
> Re-position to Act II marks, print side chair and round side table, downstage right
> Re-position c. armchair to Act II marks
> Pedestal table (from between windows) to right of center armchair
> Loveseat angled in alcove
> Magazine rack (contents made neat) to upstage center (left of bookcase)

On Poker Table:

> right (Vinnie):
>> Chips (a lot), cigarettes, matches, ash tray, with butts
>> Open, full beer can, empty clean glass, coaster
> upstage right (Speed):
>> Deck of cards, small stacks of chips
>> Empty highball glass, coaster
> upstage left (Murray):
>> Small stacks of chips
> left (Oscar):

Small stacks of chips, 2 coasters
Cigar, matches, ash tray, with butts
downstage left (Felix):
Small stacks of chips
downstage right (Roy):
Small stacks of chips, empty cup and saucer
downstage center: Bowl of pretzels

On Side Table, downstage right:
Humidor, with cigars
Brass ash tray (empty)
Green and white cigarette box

On Bookcase, right:
Record albums (Mancini and Sinatra on top)
Kitty box (cigar box) with paper money
2 fresh pots of ivy in wall brackets

On Bar:
Pure-a-tron (downstage)
Ice bucket (top on)
Leather chip box (upstage)
Corkscrew
2 decanters, full
Bottle of Scotch
Bottle of vodka
Bottle of Drambuie
4 empty clean glasses
Glass ash tray (clean)

On Coffee Table:
Breakaway cup on saucer (upstage center)
Blue ash tray (empty) (left)
Kitchen matches in cup (right)

On Pedestal Table, right of Armchair:
Cigarette lighter (check flame) (downstage left)
Gold cigarette box (downstage right)

On Telephone Table:
New lamp shade
Telephone

Phone book, with red crayon stuck in pages

Green ash tray, with butts

OFF STAGE IN KITCHEN, UPSTAGE LEFT:

On Refrigerator:

Tray, containing:

5 folded napkins

1 open, full can of beer

1 empty clean beer glass

1 glass of Scotch and water

1 clean ash tray, with cloth

1 plate, with sandwich on toast and pickle

1 glass of gin and tonic, with lime, on coaster

On Sink Drainboard:

Towel

Ladle

Silent butler, with cloth

In Sink:

Dishes and washing materials

On Back of Sink:

Air spray

On Table right :

Magazine

Silver tray, with small double vodka, Drambuie, 2 highballs

Pan, with London Broil and cooking glove (on lower level of table)

OFF STAGE LEFT:

Place top on trash can

Prop Table (for Scene 2):

Bottle of wine in paper bag

Dining table top, with dinner setting, etc.

Round tray, with dishes of potato chips, nuts, Fritos, dip

Vase with white roses

OFF STAGE RIGHT:

In Bedroom (for Scene 2):

(Clothes put back in chest)

Electric razor (on chest)

Oscar's shirt and tie (wardrobe)

OFF STAGE RIGHT:

In Bathroom (for Scene 2):

Towel folded neatly over towel rack

After-shave lotion moved downstage on sink

CHECK LIST:

All windows closed

Drapes open

Drapes over window over bookcase, right, closed

Venetian blinds all the way up

Felix's wallet in jacket, off left (wardrobe)

All doors closed, including bedroom to bathroom door, *except* kitchen door on landing slightly ajar

OFF STAGE RIGHT:

Prop Table (for Scene 2):

Vase, with gladiolus

Pot of flowers

STRIKE:

Telephone book page from bookshelf

Baseball cap from chair, downstage right

Air spray from bar

Telephone book from downstage left table

Saucer from coffee table

Pants from floor, downstage left

Sneakers from floor, downstage left

Pieces of broken cup from floor on landing

Green vase from chest on landing

SET:

Vase, with gladiolus on bookcase upstage right

Pot of flowers on bar

Move magazine rack to left of loveseat

Vase, with white roses on chest on landing

Move one downstage dining chair to left of wall jog upstage center

On Dining Table:

　　Table top with dinner setting, tablecloth, flowers, candles, etc.

On Chair at Wall Jog:

　　Felix's jacket with wallet containing pictures (wardrobe)

On Table right *of Armchair:*

　　Bowl of potato chips

On Coffee Table:

　　Bowl of nuts

　　Round tray, with bowl of Fritos and bowl of dip

CHECK:

　　Position of armchair to couch

　　Drapes closed

　　Venetian blinds all the way up

　　Windows closed

　　All doors closed

Off left:

　　Bottle of wine in paper bag

Off upstage right:

　　Electric razor

　　Shirt and tie

Off downstage right:

　　Bathroom: Bottle of after-shave lotion

ACT THREE

STRIKE:

>Dinner set up from dining table
>
>Bowls of dip, nuts, crackers, potato chips
>
>Two vases and one pot of flowers
>
>Tray with four drinks
>
>Standing lamp (elec.)

RE-SET:

>Poker table, downstage right on marks
>
>2 kitchen chairs, right and left of table (pushed in close)
>
>2 dining chairs upstage right and upstage left of poker table
>
>1 dining chair left against upstage center wall jog
>
>1 dining chair downstage against upstage center wall jog
>
>Loveseat in above (centered between windows)
>
>Magazine rack right of loveseat
>
>Reposition armchair and pedestal table to Act Three marks

>*On Bookshelf, upstage right:*
>
>>Chip box, with chips (on pile of record albums)
>>
>>Kitty box (cigar box) empty
>>
>>2 decks of cards
>>
>>Cigarettes and matches
>>
>>2 ash trays

>*On Round Table, downstage right:*
>
>>Magazine (on humidor)

>*On Bar:*
>
>>Bottle of whisky
>>
>>4 empty, clean glasses
>>
>>Air spray
>>
>>2 decanters, puritron, ash tray, ice bucket

>*On Pedestal Table, right of Armchair:*
>
>>Gold cigarette box

>*On Coffee Table:*
>
>>2 sports magazines (right)
>>
>>Green ash tray, with butts (left)
>>
>>Wooden matches in cup (left)

On Telephone Table:
> Blue ash tray, clean

On Chest (on landing):
> Green vase

OFF STAGE IN KITCHEN, UPSTAGE LEFT:

Pile of good cookware, on drainboard

Tray, with plate linguini, fork, spoon, napkin, on refrigerator

Pile of pots and pans (for crash sound), on refrigerator 6-pack of beer, unopened bags of Fritos and pretzels, on floor between doors

OFF STAGE LEFT:

Prop Table:
> New York Post
>
> Cigar in wrapper
>
> Key case, with detachable key

OFF STAGE RIGHT:

In Bedroom, upstage right:
> Vacuum cleaner, with long cord, plugged in (practical) (elec.)

OFF STAGE RIGHT:

In Bedroom, right:
> Suitcase
>
> 2 suits on hangers, in plastic bag (on hook)
>
> Felix's jacket on hook (wardrobe)
>
> Crash sound

CHECK:

Cord on vacuum cleaner

Position of chairs at table

Drapes closed

All doors closed, *except* upstage right bedroom

Felix—paper money in pocket

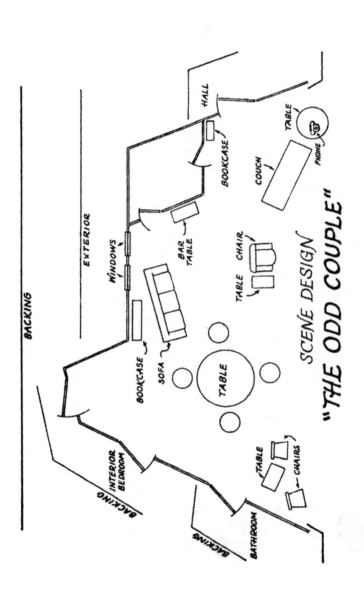

SCENE DESIGN
"THE ODD COUPLE"

"THE ODD COUPLE"
SCENE DESIGN